# Death of a Dean

# Death of a Dean

Hazel Holt

cp
coffeetownpress
Seattle, WA

Published by Coffeetown Press
PO Box 70515
Seattle, WA 98127

For more information go to: www.coffeetownpress.com



Cover design by Sabrina Sun
Photograph of JoJo the Cat by Nancy Johnson

Death of a Dean


First published in Great Britain by Macmillan London, Limited, 1996.

ISBN: 978-1-60381-142-2 (Trade Paper)
ISBN: 978-1-60381-143-9 (eBook)

Printed in the United States of America

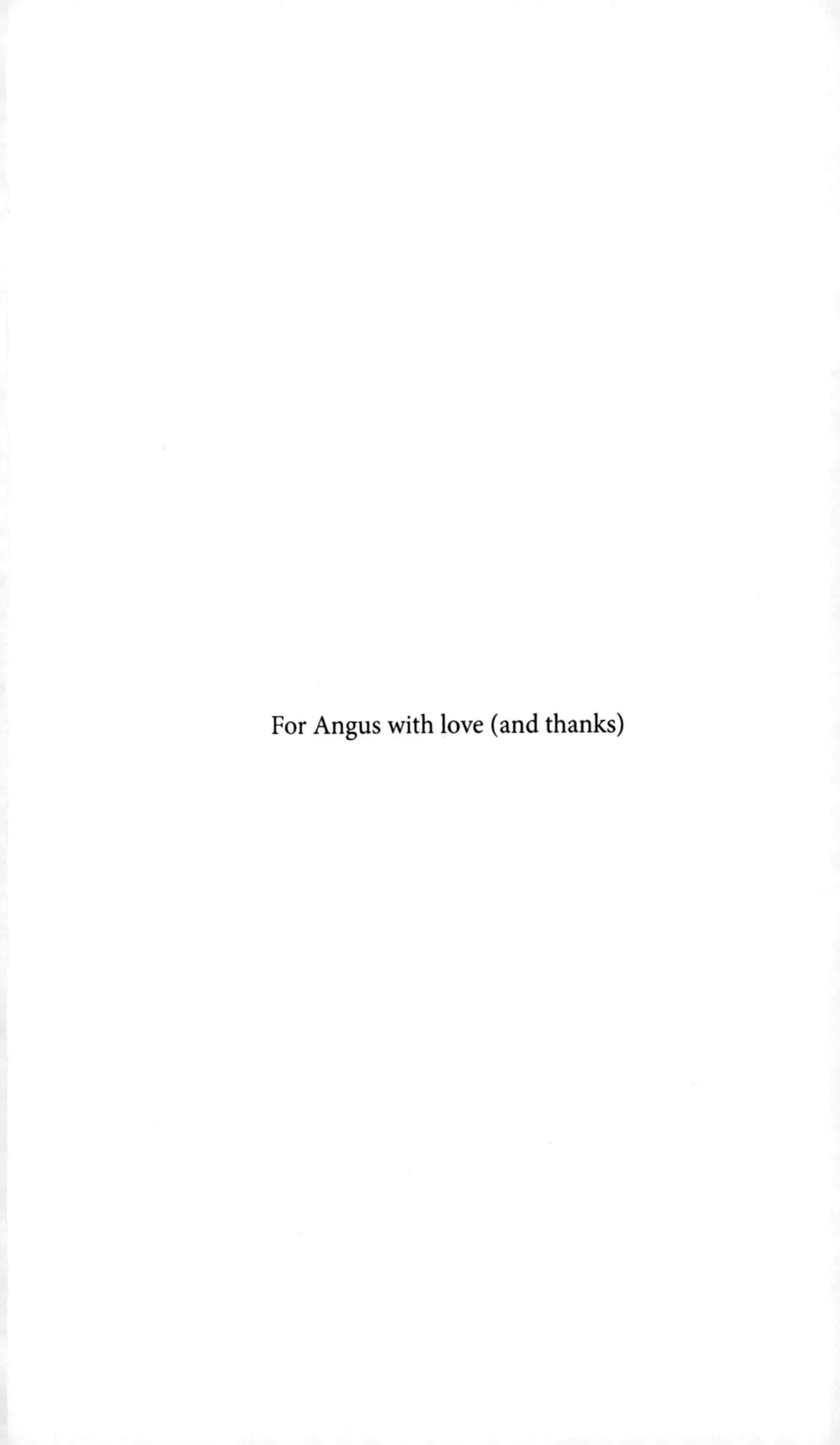

For Angus with love (and thanks)

# 1

"I'll put him on your sleeve," the young man said. "The Harris hawk thinks humans are his kith and kin, so he won't stand on your bare arm because he's afraid of hurting you with his feet."

He transferred the bird gently from his glove and I was amazed to find how light it was, a barely perceptible presence on my arm. The hawk stared at me and his great golden eye seemed to grow until I felt I was consumed by it and could see nothing else. It shook its head and the bells attached to its jesses gave out a tiny sound, faint and metallic as if from far away, another place, another age, perhaps.

" 'If I do prove her haggard' "—David's splendid actor's voice beside me—" 'though that her jesses were my dear heart's strings, I'd whistle her off and let her down the wind to prey at fortune.' " Then, having apparently exhausted his knowledge of hawks and hawking, he looked at his watch and said, "Well, Sheila darling, if you can bear to leave your little medieval fantasy world, how about a delicious cup of *tea*?"

I laughed and raised my arm gently so that the hawk moved down it and back once more onto the young man's leather glove.

"Thank you," I said, "that was wonderful." I turned to David. "Can we see him fly just once more?"

The young man cast off the bird, which flew high into the sky, soaring, so that it hurt one's eyes to follow it. Then it flew down onto the ornate Tudor chimney pot and sat watching us.

"It's all right," the young man said. "He'll come to the lure, he's not had much to eat today."

He whirled the lure around and sure enough the hawk flew at it, swooping down almost to the ground, then up and off again into the blue air. Several times the lure flew and each time the bird came nearer, until he finally took it and stood with his foot on the dead baby chick, tearing off the pale yellow down.

"This is the bit I *don't* like," I said. "We'll go now and get that cup of tea."

We strolled down the gravel path, past the row of hawks on their perches behind the low fence. Those that were unhooded regarded us impassively, except for one buzzard that pulled at its leash and uttered a continuous mewing cry.

Whenever I'm in Stratford I always have to go to Mary Arden's house at Wilmcote—not just for the house, though I love it dearly, but for the hawks that are kept there. I like to watch them fly and listen to the young man—a true falconer with tremendous enthusiasm and a burning desire to communicate his passion—talking about the birds and all the tradition and ritual that surround them. Today I was lucky. Because it was early in the year we'd been the only people there so I'd had a private view, as it were.

I took David's arm. "That was very noble of you," I said. "I hope you weren't too bored, but I do love them so!"

"Whatever turns you on, dear," he replied amiably. "Although I must say that birds always seem to me particularly *sinister* creatures—something to do with having eyes on each side of their head, I suppose."

"But you must admit they're very handsome?"

"Handsome is as handsome does, as Nana used to say," he said repressively. "And I'm perfectly sure they'd peck your eyes out as soon as look at you."

"You may be right," I said, "but I can't help having this *thing* about them."

"*I* blame T.H. White," David said. "You were perfectly sensible until you read *The Sword in the Stone.* Ah, here's the tearoom. Now we must both have immense cream teas and then we can just have an omelette and some salad for supper."

It's always a treat to go and stay with David. I've known him forever and we share so many memories. He and his brother Francis are the children of my mother's dearest friend in Taviscombe and their father was our family solicitor, so we saw quite a lot of each other when we were growing up. Well, David and I did, being the same age. Francis was a good bit older, nearer to my brother Jeremy in age, but they weren't close. Francis (who was never called Frank, even by his schoolfellows) was a difficult boy, remote and somehow unfriendly. We were all rather surprised when he went into the Church, since he never seemed to have those qualities of compassion and humanity that one would have thought fairly basic necessities for such a calling. However, he's done very well, prospered even, if such a word can be used for a churchman, and is now the Dean of Culminster.

David went on the stage. I think his parents were a little disappointed since, in those days, it was not considered a "proper job," but they were loving parents and they supported him (financially as well) for several years until he established himself in the theater. He never played the great roles, but he was a fine Enobarbus, a lyrical Orsino, a splendidly devious Claudius and a noble Banquo. But even to those who never saw him in the theater, the name of David Beaumont became what is known as a household word. He was Inspector Ivor in the television series *Ivor Investigates*, which ran for years and years. That was the trouble, really, because when the series finally ended, poor David, like others before him, was so thoroughly typecast that he found it difficult to know where to go from there. A couple of unsuccessful theatrical ventures and a perfectly dreadful situation comedy and he found that he was no longer—what's the phrase they use?—"bankable." It didn't help, too, that his agent was getting old and no longer really interested ("And you see, dear, you can't change your agent when you're on a *down*, can you?") so that the work simply didn't come.

People who still thought of him as a "name" didn't consider him for the small parts he'd have been glad enough to take and, apart from the occasional voice-over for a commercial, he hasn't been offered anything for quite a while now.

Fortunately, in the days of his affluence he'd bought a flat in Highgate and a small cottage in Stratford. Lydia, his ex-wife, took the flat but David had managed to hang onto the cottage, which is where he lives now. It's a very desirable property, being immediately opposite the Memorial Theater in the heart of the town and David loves it with a consuming passion. It's become the one fixed thing in his life, a substitute, I suppose, for work, marriage and family. It is also a minute source of income, since he takes in lodgers, and there's usually a young man, attached to the Royal Shakespeare Company in some capacity, in the only spare room. Any guests (and David is very hospitable) have David's room, while he sleeps in some discomfort on a very old sofa bed in the sitting room.

"Right," David said briskly as the tea arrived, "will you be mother?" He watched me critically as I struggled with a dribbling teapot and burned my fingers on the metal hot-water jug. "Now then, have a delicious scone—I think they're homemade, though I'm not sure about the jam." He stirred the bright red preserve with a spoon. "Not strawberry, I fear, nor raspberry, plum, perhaps, would you say? Evesham being so close, I think we may deduce the presence of plums."

"So when," I asked, "am I going to see your new lodger?"

"Julian? Oh, have I told you? He's almost the *perfect*

lodger—one simply never sees him. He's got a couple of small parts this season, as well as walk-ons—one of the Ambassadors in *Hamlet* (lovely for him that they're doing the full version) and Seton in the Scottish play—so he's out in the evenings, and during the day they have all these workshops and voice classes and so on—absolutely splendid, never in!"

"Oh, I hope I do catch a glimpse," I said. David's lodgers are always delightful young men with beautiful manners and sometimes they become quite famous and I'm able to say, "Of course I knew him when ..." Often they owe part of their success to David, who, as well as being the most kindly and generous of people, has a passionate devotion to the theater and gives a great deal of his time and energy to helping the young, both by advice and by digging up contacts for them in the theater that he would never dream of using for himself. Sometimes in the days of their success they remember what they owe him. Sometimes they do not.

"Shall we go and see him?" I asked. "Not perhaps four hours of that particular *Hamlet*, but I wouldn't mind adding another *Macbeth* to my collection. I think it's fifteen—no, sixteen, if you count that fantastic Peter O'Toole performance that I adored and you hated."

I did see the elusive Julian, just emerging from the kitchen as we got back. He looked a little anxious.

"I do hope it's all right, and you did say to help myself, only I felt I wanted just a little something before the matinee today, something light, you know, so I had a couple of boiled eggs. I'm afraid I took the last two." He was a tall boy in his early twenties, with a lot of fair hair and great gray eyes that he now fixed on David.

"No, that's fine, no problem," David said amiably.

"I'll get some more in tomorrow, but there hasn't been time today—I must dash now or I won't be back for the half hour. I had to pop back here to get some more cotton wool, I've run out." He turned to me. "It's brilliant living just across the road from the theater like this, I'm frightfully lucky—the others are simply *green* with envy!"

"Forgive me," David said, "this is Sheila, Sheila Malory, the old friend I told you about who's staying for a few days—so please don't hog the bathroom as you usually do!" He smiled at Julian, who smiled back, a dazzling smile that encompassed us both.

"Lovely to see you, Sheila," he said. "I'll catch up with you both later. Must be off to work now, do forgive me." Another smile and he was gone.

"Oh dear, bang goes the omelette," David said ruefully. "It'll have to be sardines or something."

"A very personable young man," I said. "Is he any good?"

"I think he has distinct possibilities," he replied. "He wants to *learn* and that's always a good sign, don't you think? Anyway, you shall judge for yourself. Seton is *quite* a test of anyone's ability!"

It was, actually, a typical RSC production of *Macbeth*. Lots of swirling smoke and leather armor and those World War Two greatcoats that seem to be an indispensable part of their wardrobe (I swear I caught sight of them once in a production of *Love's Labor's Lost*). Oh yes, and that peculiar music they seem so fond of, rather twangy and atonal and played on obscure instruments. Birnham Wood came to Dunsinane by means of back-projection, and I've never seen so much gore as when a rather overparted Macduff held up a dripping Thing, alleged to be the head of Macbeth but fortunately unidentifiable.

"So what did you think?" David asked as we sat by the dying embers of the fire in his tiny sitting room.

"Well, he remembered his lines and didn't trip over the furniture—and Glamis Castle *was* rather overfurnished, I thought, rather as if Lady Macbeth had been to some sort of Gothic ideal homes exhibition! And at least he was *audible*—not like that dreadful Banquo, who might just as well have been a ghost from the beginning for all I heard!"

We sat there until quite late, enjoyably picking the production to pieces. After a bit, Julian came in and we told him how good he'd been and he told us how Seton really was quite a *significant* character if you looked at the play as a whole and we all had a nice cup of tea and Julian told us the latest RSC gossip and we all had a tiny whiskey just as a nightcap and after a while I left them to it and went to bed. It's sad, really, how I can't stay up late as I used to. Perhaps, as a middle-aged widow living in a small West Country town, I don't have a lot to stay up late for, so I've somehow got out of the habit.

The next day David and I had a little wander around the town, which is something I never tire of doing. Even this early in the season there were the ubiquitous coachloads of tourists, shrieking French schoolchildren, silent Japanese photographing everything in sight, just in case it turned out to be relevant, and the occasional American couple, like the first swallows, an earnest of the flocks to come. But Stratford has, for me, this amazing ability to absorb all these crowds and still remain (in spite of the souvenir shops and that horrid new Shakespeare Centre that disfigures the Birthplace) the small market town it always was, and the half-timbered Smiths and Pizza Hut are so delightfully absurd that I'm quite sure Shakespeare would have enjoyed them as much as I do.

We strolled down Chapel Lane, past the school and along the river, up to the church. It's very touristy now and you have to pay to look at the monument, but that well-known but somehow mysterious bust and the enigmatic inscription never fail to give me a little thrill of excitement.

"I'm glad all that nonsense about opening the grave came to nothing," I said as we walked down the tree-shadowed path through the churchyard. "Even if they'd found something really thrilling, it would have been wrong. They *would* have been cursed, I feel sure!"

"Oh well, the city fathers would never allow it, in case there was something there that proved that the plays were really written by Marlowe or the earl of Southampton," David said.

"Of *course* Shakespeare wrote them," I said indignantly. "You only have to *be* in Stratford to know that. There are living references to things in the plays everywhere you go!"

David laughed. "You needn't be so fierce—*I* don't need convincing! Right, now, where next? Halls Croft, I suppose."

"Of course."

We turned right out of the churchyard and walked a little way along the wide street until we came to Halls Croft, the house where Dr. Hall, Shakespeare's son-in-law, lived. If a grateful nation ever offered me the gift of a house, this would be the one I'd choose. It's a very handsome building, with pale silvery weathered beams let into the mellow brick and, inside, black beams on white walls, highly polished sloping wooden floors and a splendid staircase. There is a solidity, a sense of achievement and quiet pride that is very comforting somehow, a feeling of continuity, that life goes on and will continue to do so, steadily and imperturbably, a tribute to the durability of humankind.

We walked through the house and into the garden.

"I don't suppose they'd let me be scattered here?" I said regretfully as we walked across the grass beside the great mulberry tree, leaning almost parallel with the ground and supported by a fork. "Still, Michael's promised to donate a memorial seat for me with a plaque."

"Don't be morbid, dear."

"I'm not. I like to think that something of me would be here after I've gone. Do you think it's warm enough for us to have a little sit-down?"

We sat on one of the benches ("In memory of James Austin of Philadelphia, who loved Stratford and this place"). To our right a gardener was at work on one of the long herbaceous borders that later in the year would be a blaze of color, one of the glories of all the Shakespeare houses. A thrush perched on the sundial by the little arbor and began to sing its song, startlingly loud in the stillness of the garden.

" 'With heigh! with heigh! the thrush and the jay,' " David said. "A difficult play, *The Winter's Tale*, with all that *chronology* going on in the interval!"

I drew in a deep breath. "Oh, isn't it gorgeous here! How lucky you are to live in Stratford! And how lucky I am that I can come and visit you!"

"It may not be for much longer," David said.

For a moment I didn't take in what he'd said, then I looked at him in amazement.

"David! What on earth do you mean?"

"Well, I wasn't going to tell you—I didn't want to spoil your visit. But things are getting pretty bad. Financially, that is. I may have to sell the house."

"Oh, no!" I cried. "Surely there's some other way? How about the bank? Can't you get a loan, or a mortgage on the house?"

"I'm afraid it's the bank that's pressing for money," he replied. "I've got a pretty horrendous overdraft. And the house is mortgaged already."

"Oh, David!"

"It all started with that wretched accountant—you remember—who made a balls-up of my tax when I was earning a decent whack in the *Ivor Investigates* days. I never really got straight from that—had to borrow from the bank, and then the work didn't come, and one's got to live ..."

"And you've always been far too generous to other people," I interjected.

"And Eddy got himself into a bit of a mess."

Eddy is David's son, grown up now and off heaven knows where with some pop group. I didn't think David had seen him for ages.

"Eddy? What happened? Where is he?"

"He *was* in Paris, singing in a club there, but then he got mixed up with some rather weird people—drugs, I think, though he didn't actually say ... Anyway, he came back to London."

He paused and sat for a moment, apparently looking at a sparrow that was hopping around our feet hoping for crumbs.

"And he wanted money, of course," I said.

"He was pretty scared of these people, whoever they were," David said, "so what could I do? He *is* my son—you know you'd have done the same for Michael."

"Yes, I suppose so," I said slowly, "though, thank heavens, Michael is a model citizen and far more likely to get *me* out of a scrape than the other way round!"

David laughed. "You make him sound like the most dreadful prig and really he's a very amusing young man."

"Yes, I know, I'm frightfully lucky—especially since he's chosen to work in Taviscombe and share a home with his highly demanding mother! But it's unfair that you should have Eddy's money problems as well as your own. Nothing from Leo, I suppose?"

Leo is David's agent.

"There was some talk of a couple of days' filming on location in the Cotswolds, something about a canal barge—it would have been very handy, but it fell through."

"Leo made a muddle, I suppose—he really is the end!" I exclaimed. "What else is there?" I thought for a moment. "Could you sell something?" I suggested tentatively.

David has a fantastic number of books on the theater, covering every inch of wall space in the cottage and piled high in corners. He also has a lot of prints and other theatrical memorabilia. It's a remarkable collection and people come from all over the country to consult it. It's always known jokingly as The Bequest, because David says he intends to leave it to some worthy institution.

"No," he replied. "Not if you mean The Bequest. You know how I feel about that."

"But if it's a choice between that and losing the cottage..."

"Yes, well, I know." He shrugged. "And even if I did, I don't suppose I'd get all that much for it—you know how it is when you try to sell things."

We sat in silence for a while. The beauty of the day and the surroundings seemed suddenly dimmed.

"I don't suppose Francis would help?" I asked. "After all, there is the house."

The house is the large house in Taviscombe where the Beaumonts used to live. It's in what's known as a very favorable position on West Hill, overlooking the sea, and must be worth quite a lot of money. Mrs. Beaumont died relatively young and David's father was looked after in his declining years by the boys' old nanny, who was deeply devoted to him. When Mr. Beaumont died and the will was read it was discovered, to everyone's amazement, that the house was left to her for her lifetime, and only at her death would Francis and David inherit. What money there was was left for the upkeep of the house.

Francis, who has a very keen financial sense and is one of the trustees, tried very hard to find some way around it. He offered the old woman another house, but she stubbornly refused to move, saying that if Mr. Beaumont had wanted it and had written it down in his will it would be wrong to do anything else.

David sighed. "Oh, I know," he said. "It is provoking. Just the other day Francis told me that the trustees had a *fantastic* offer from someone who wanted to turn it into a nursing home."

"Taviscombe can always do with another of those," I said, "considering the average age of the population! And it really is ridiculous to think of her living all alone in that enormous house. Can *nothing* be done about it?"

" 'Fraid not, you know how it is."

"Yes, I suppose if anyone could have broken the trust somehow it would have been Francis! Couldn't *you* speak to her, though? You were always her favorite."

"I did try," he said, "but poor old Nana, once she gets something into her head, then that's that, and she's utterly convinced that by staying there—and she's always going on about how inconvenient it is!—she's doing what my father wanted. Practically Holy Writ!"

"Well, he certainly wouldn't have wanted you to lose your home!" I said indignantly. "That's what you get, having an old nurse called Nana, like the St. Bernard in *Peter Pan*!"

"It's a great pity she isn't a St. Bernard," David said morosely, "then we could have her put down."

# 2

David wasn't an early riser and, to my great surprise, Julian had gone out jogging.

"Acting's a very *physical* thing, you do see, Sheila," Julian had said earnestly as he edged past me in the little hall on his way to the front door, "so keeping the body really fit is *just* as important as, say, voice production. Don't you agree?"

I stood in the tiny kitchen waiting for the kettle to boil and admiring a fine greenfinch that was jockeying for position with the blue tits on the bird feeder outside the window. I craned forward for a better look and saw a little siskin hopping about underneath the feeder waiting for crumbs of peanut to fall onto the path beneath. The analogy with Life was unpleasantly strong so I turned away and busied myself with slices of bread and the toaster.

When I'd finished my toast, I perched on a kitchen stool drinking my coffee and leafing through one of the copies of *Play Pictorial* (1932 Gielgud in *Musical Chairs*), which, instead of china, filled the shelves of the oak dresser. Although the really valuable items of David's collection (a pair of Irving's pince-nez, a golden chain Forbes Robertson had worn as Hamlet, a ribbon knot that was part of Ellen Terry's costume as Beatrice, the silver casket from Beerbohm Tree's *Merchant of Venice*, a carte de visite of Modjeska and other treasures) were in the sitting room, many other items of theatrical interest gave the kitchen an unexpected look. As well as playbills and prints of obscure and long-dead actors, there was, on the walls, a pictorial record of David's career, framed programs, caricatures, stills from films and television plays, and, inevitably, a picture of David as Inspector Ivor, leaning on the bonnet of the splendid old racing green Bentley that became almost as famous as he did.

I got up from the stool and went over to look at it. Though not, as they say, conventionally handsome, he has a good actor's face—a high forehead, a strong chin and a rather splendidly aquiline nose. In the picture his hair was thicker and his figure slighter, but he's still in pretty good shape. After Lydia left him we all thought he'd marry again, but although, in that first year, he had several relationships of a temporary nature, he then seemed to retreat into himself emotionally. He and Lydia had originally come together when she appeared in one of the episodes of *Ivor Investigates*. She'd already made something of a name for herself on television, playing sensitive young girls. She had, then, a heart-shaped face with great gray eyes, and a fall of long, blond hair that gave her the look of a vulnerable child. Which she certainly wasn't.

I never cared for Lydia—"a calculating little piece," Peter, my husband, called her—but she was always perfectly civil to me and, while his marriage lasted, I didn't see all that much of David anyway. I don't really know what went wrong.

"Well, you see, dear," David said by way of explanation, "we were both so busy that we didn't have time to notice that we weren't happy, and when we did it was too late."

As David's career declined so hers took off. She had several successes with the National—a lovely Perdita and an interesting Ophelia—but, as the years went by, suitable parts were harder to find. By a great piece of good fortune she was offered a part in a popular soap opera and very sensibly took it and has remained with it ever since, and now it is she who is something of a national institution.

She married again—twice—and Eddy (always a difficult child) had a pretty unsettled upbringing. David, I know, felt rather guilty about this, though, as I pointed out, Lydia was a perfectly kind if erratic mother, and *he* certainly wouldn't have found it easy to bring up a demanding small boy on his own. But I suppose this feeling of guilt made him particularly vulnerable to Eddy's financial demands, which came fairly frequently over the years. A charming young man when he wanted to be, but thoroughly selfish and, I always felt, totally devoid of feeling for either of his parents. I hoped in a way that, having got what he could out of David for the moment, he would drop out of his life again.

"A most extraordinary thing, darling!" David's voice behind me made me jump. He came into the kitchen waving a letter. "I've just heard from Martin."

Martin Ross was one of David's oldest friends. They had been at the Royal Academy of Dramatic Art together and both their careers had taken off at about the same time—as David became a television personality, so Martin had made his name as a director, first at Stratford, then in the commercial theater. Some years ago he'd gone to Australia, where he combined stage work with lecturing on drama at Brisbane University.

"How nice," I said. "Is he coming over on a visit?"

"No, no," David said, "well, not immediately. But, the most marvelous thing! He's been asked to help set up a Shakespeare Center here in Stratford and there's just a possibility there might be a job in it for me! Isn't it fantastic!"

"How wonderful!" I exclaimed. "Here, sit down. I'll pour you some coffee and you can tell me all about it, *slowly*. You're practically incoherent."

"Well"—David sat down at the table and began spooning sugar into the coffee I put before him—"there's this splendid Australian female, called Beth Cameron, who's absolutely potty about Shakespeare. She's also incredibly rich and has no family, so she's going to use some of her millions to found this center in Stratford—she *adores* Stratford—for the study of Shakespeare's plays in performance. It would combine acting and academic studies, so she wants an actor to run it." He took a great gulp of his coffee and continued. "She's taken a terrific shine to Martin and is asking his advice about everything and he, bless him, told her about me. Fortunately she saw my Claudius, you know, when I did that Australian tour with Alec, and she remembered me. So Martin told her that I had administrative experience—when I ran those seasons at Kidderminster Rep—and, of course, about The Bequest and living here in Stratford, and she sounded very impressed!"

"Oh David! How perfect!"

"Isn't it, though!" he said excitedly. "It would be the most *wonderful* job, something I'd love doing."

"And you're so good with the young," I said. "And there's all your experience and enthusiasm—there's so *much* you could teach them!"

"It's the most marvelous opportunity!" David's eyes were shining and he looked at least ten years younger. "A sort of once-in-a-lifetime thing!"

"Isn't it!" I agreed. "And it's simply made for you."

We sat and smiled at each other and I poured us each another cup of coffee.

"So when will she decide—this Cameron woman?" I asked.

"She's coming over with Martin later this year," David replied, "and she'll obviously be interviewing a lot of people."

"Oh, but when she sees you and this cottage and The Bequest and everything—well, she'll absolutely *have* to give the job to you. I mean, what more could she want!"

"Bless you, dear! But Martin really does seem to think that my being here in Stratford and everything will be the real clincher. God! I do hope so. It would be the solution to my financial problems as well as being the most heavenly job. I mean, the salary won't be enormous but it'll be *regular* and quite enough to let me pay off the overdraft and ..." He broke off. "Oh God, the overdraft!"

"What about it?" I asked. "You'll be able to pay it off, like you said."

"No, but don't you see!" he groaned. "The bank's pressing me for that money *now*. By the time Beth Cameron's over here I'll have had to get out. I won't have the cottage, I might even have to leave Stratford altogether. Certainly my name in the town, financially speaking, will be mud. *That's* not going to impress her!"

"But won't the bank give you more time?" I asked. "I mean, if you explain to them about this fabulous job?"

"Yes, dear, but I haven't actually *got* it, have I? I don't see them giving me unlimited credit on the strength of something that *might* come off, do you?"

"Oh, no! How cruel! There must be some way. Can't you borrow from someone else?"

"A loan shark, do you mean?" David looked at me quizzically. "I don't think I want to go down *that* particular primrose path to the everlasting bonfire, thank you, dear!"

"No, silly," I replied, "but what about Francis? He must be absolutely *rolling* and he can have your share of the house as security—he is a trustee or something, isn't he?"

David grimaced. "I don't really like the thought of asking Francis for anything. You know how scornful he's always been about the theater. It was bad enough when I was successful ... Anyway, I haven't let him know how things are nowadays. I mean, he's not exactly au fait with the theatrical scene. As far as he knows I'm still the most tremendously sought-after character actor in the business. I'd hate to have to admit that things are—well, you know!"

"I do know, David dear, but you really mustn't let your pride stand in the way of this fantastic chance. I do so agree that being patronized by Francis would be horrid, but if that's the only way ..."

"I suppose you're right," David sighed, "there is no other way. But it's not going to be easy."

That afternoon when I got back from shopping David greeted me gloomily.

"I wrote the letter," he said. "It's so sycophantic I feel really *sick*."

"Never mind," I said cheerfully, "let's hope it does the trick. Look, I got smoked salmon and a rather nice Chardonnay to celebrate the job."

I returned home to Taviscombe before David had a reply from Francis and it was, in fact, a full week before I heard from him. I was just glumly surveying a pile of newly washed clothes (one stuffs them into the washing machine, recklessly disregarding the fact that they'll all have to be ironed eventually) when the telephone rang. It was David. As soon as I heard his voice I knew that his appeal to Francis hadn't been successful.

"*Cash flow*, darling, *liquidity*, all the old financial clichés! Something about not wishing to sell shares with the market in its present state. And quite insufferable, as always. Just listen to this! 'I was, you may remember, deeply unhappy about your choice of career, from the very beginning. Indeed, I expressed my views quite emphatically to Father at the time. Alas.' Only Francis could use 'alas' in a letter! Where was I? Oh yes. 'Alas, he chose not to exercise his parental authority and forbid you to embark on a path that was all too likely to lead to debt and disaster. Indeed, I believe he positively encouraged you. I have to say, I am glad he did not live to see that his trust in your ability to make a career for yourself in such a risky profession (if so it can be called) was sadly misplaced.' Pompous fool! I won't go on. There's a lot more like that—sanctimonious rubbish. And he signs himself 'Your affectionate brother,' if you please."

"Oh, David!" I cried, "I'm so sorry. What an absolute *bastard* Francis is. Talk about unchristian! He must have some money not tied up in shares, and Joan has money of her own. I'm sure he could help if he wanted to. It's not as if you're asking him to *give* it to you, he *knows* you'll pay him back."

David sighed. "Oh well, I suppose it was worth a try, but I must confess I always feel about five inches tall when I get one of Francis's sardonic little homilies. He's always treated me like that, ever since we were children. 'I don't think you ought to do *that*, David, you know how upset Mother would be if she knew'—and you knew just *how* she'd find out. Or, 'I'm only telling you for your own good, you'll thank me one day.' Yuk!"

"Oh yes," I said, "and doesn't he love to put one down! I remember, when I was about fifteen, I persuaded Mother to buy me this wildly unsuitable dress—bright red and definitely *slinky*—to wear at the Chapmans' Christmas party (you remember they were rather grand affairs) and Francis was there. He gave me the most *icy* stare and said that he was astonished that my mother had allowed me to make such a vulgar exhibition of myself. You *know* how fragile one's self-confidence is at that age—I spent the rest of the evening hiding my shame in the conservatory!"

"I've never understood how he's got on so amazingly in the church," David said sourly. "He certainly doesn't embody many of the Christian virtues."

"Oh, but he's such a wizard with money," I replied. "Look how he's improved the financial situation of every parish he's ever been connected with and now, as dean, he's tremendously involved in fund-raising for the cathedral—the roof's quietly disintegrating, of course, as well as the usual running expenses. I know the bishop's deeply impressed with what he's done already. That's what's so *sickening*. I'm sure he could have found a way out for you if he'd really put his mind to it. But he's so smug and self-satisfied ...."

"He's never really liked me, of course," David said meditatively, "because I was always our parents' favorite."

"Well, you were a lovable little boy—he was always a calculating little monster."

"Still, his parishioners seemed quite devoted."

"They're mostly female," I explained, "and middle-aged, and he is what is known as a fine figure of a man, tall and rather distinguished with all that gray hair and those very blue eyes."

"I *suppose*," David said doubtfully.

"And he can turn on a sort of aloof charm when he wants to. I suppose that's what attracted Joan."

Joan is Francis's wife. She is a shy, retiring woman, rather dim, really, in appearance and personality. It is generally accepted that Francis married her because her father was a bishop and she had inherited a considerable amount of money from her mother. They have two children, very much under their father's thumb. Adrian, the eldest, is an accountant and Mary is a librarian, both nervous, uncertain creatures, whom I've never heard express any positive opinion of their own—certainly not when their father's present.

"Poor Joan," David said. "Incredibly enough, she seems to adore him, always saying how marvelous he is. And he treats her like some sort of slave. Quite extraordinary!"

"Oh, some women are born doormats! So, if Francis is a washout we'll have to think of something else. Actually, if it would help, I could lend you a couple of thousand ..."

"No, dear, absolutely not," David said firmly. "It's sweet of you and I'm deeply touched and grateful, but I really couldn't."

"But that's what friends are for," I protested.

"You are an angel to think of it," he said warmly, "and if it was just a couple of thousand I'd say thank you very much, because I know you're offering it as a true friend, bless you.

But I'm afraid I need an awful lot more than that."

"Well, remember it's there if you want it."

"I'll remember. Of course, if only poor old Nana would pop off it would solve all my problems, but she looks like outliving us all."

"Yes, I saw her in Boots the other day," I said, "and I must admit she did look pretty spry."

"Oh well," David said glumly, "I'll just have to rob a bank or something—I'm sure, after all those years playing Inspector Ivor, I should know enough about police procedure to avoid being caught."

"Better not," I replied. "You know you couldn't resist giving a *performance*, right over the top, and you'd be recognized immediately."

"I expect you're right. Oh well, I'd better have another go at Leo. A couple of good commercials could put me right."

"Yes, of course. Good luck."

But we both knew that that possibility was very remote indeed.

# 3

Actually, I ran into Francis's wife, Joan, the very next day at a bring-and-buy sale run by the Friends of Culminster Cathedral. I was more or less shanghaied into going by my friend Anthea, who is very into church affairs.

"You needn't bring," she said briskly, "but you can buy."

We went in her car, laden with homemade cakes, pots of jam and rooted cuttings, which was a nuisance because it meant I was dependent on her for transport and would have to stay to the bitter end, with no chance of slipping away quietly halfway through.

Culminster is a pleasant town—a city, I suppose, since it has a cathedral. Its prosperity was founded on the wool trade and the rich merchants left a legacy of many fine Georgian houses and civic buildings. There is also a small but very beautiful assembly room, where the daughters of those merchants showed off their finery and hunted for husbands at subscription balls. This is where the sale was being held. As we went in, the astonishing volume of noise produced by a number of (mainly) female voices assaulted my ears and I could hardly hear what Anthea was saying.

"I said," she repeated, "I'll go and take these things over to Beryl—she's got the stall set up already. You go and have a wander around. I'll see you later for a cup of coffee."

I set off to do my duty. I bought a pot of homemade lemon curd (something I always find too fiddly to make myself), a slightly lopsided ginger cake and a small camellia in a pot. I was just trying to accommodate these items safely in my shopping bag when I was aware of someone standing beside me trying to attract my attention. It was Joan Beaumont.

"Oh, hello, Joan," I said. "Lovely to see you—it's been ages."

"Oh, Sheila," she said, her soft voice difficult to hear in the general hubbub, "I'd be so grateful for a word, if you can spare the time."

She sounded really quite agitated and I wondered what on earth she wanted.

"Look," I said, "I can't hear a thing in this noise, let's go and have a cup of coffee."

I led the way into a small room leading off the main hall where tables and chairs were laid out and a long trestle with plates of small cakes, cups and saucers and the ubiquitous urn from which a large woman in a hat was dispensing coffee.

"I'll get them," I said, putting my shopping bag down on one of the chairs. "Would you like a cake or anything?"

"Oh, no thank you, Sheila, just coffee will be lovely."

I was unable to resist the temptation of a slice of caramel-covered shortbread. Unfortunately, it was very brittle and pieces flew all over the table when I tried to attack it with a fork.

"Oh, bother the thing," I said. "I'll just have to eat it with my fingers! Now, what did you want to talk to me about?"

Joan took a nervous sip of her coffee.

"We're having a rather grand auction in aid of the Cathedral Restoration Fund," she said, "and I'm afraid I've got to organize it."

"Oh, hard luck," I exclaimed. "I had to do ours for the Red Cross in Taviscombe and that was only a very small affair. A big one for the cathedral must be really horrendous!"

"I didn't want to do it at all, but being the dean's wife,

people expect one," she said earnestly. "I'm not very good at getting people to do things and I keep making such awful muddles and Francis gets so angry ..."

"Yes, well," I said, wiping the caramel off my fingers with a tissue, "it's really hard work and you need a lot of help from other people. I was frightfully lucky—everyone rallied around splendidly, collecting items to be auctioned and so on. And we had Tom Benson to do the actual sale—he's our local auctioneer, very jolly, full of jokes. He was terrific at getting the bidding up. We made a couple of thousand pounds, far more than we expected."

"Yes, Anthea was telling me what a great success it was. So I wondered ..." Her voice trailed off.

"Yes?"

"I wondered if you could *possibly* give me a hand with ours—since you know how it should be done. It would be *such* a help and I'd be so grateful ...."

She looked up at me with the kind of appealing look in her sad brown eyes that I can never resist in my spaniel, Tess.

Knowing perfectly well the aggravation I was letting myself in for, I heard my voice saying, "Yes, of course I will. I'd be delighted."

"Oh, Sheila, that's *so* kind. I wonder ... do you think you could come over one day next week—the time's going on—and have a talk about it? Come to tea."

I got my diary out. "Let me see. Would Tuesday be any use?"

"Oh yes, yes, that would be lovely. Francis is always in for tea on Tuesdays and I know he'd love to see you."

The thought of tea with Francis Beaumont—especially after his shabby treatment of David—was definitely not an inducement, but I murmured something polite and, after a little desultory conversation, Joan suddenly remembered that, as the dean's wife, she was due to draw the winning raffle ticket for the usual bottle of Bristol Cream sherry and went away.

I sat for a while over another cup of coffee thinking how awful it must be to be married to Francis, especially for a little mouselike creature like Joan. Even after all these years, she still seemed to be as ineffectual as ever in what must be the very demanding role of the dean's wife. And I can't imagine that Francis is very supportive—or patient, even. It's not as if the children were any help, being similarly mouselike themselves. It would take a really strong-minded person to stand up to Francis—even David, I know, finds him pretty daunting. I very much hoped that, since I was now committed to helping with this wretched auction, Francis would not be too closely involved in it.

Anthea broke into these thoughts.

"Oh, *there* you are! Can you come and lend a hand? Beryl has to go now to pick up her grandchildren from school and there's still quite a bit left on the stall."

I knew I'd regret my impulsive offer to help Joan and by the evening I was cursing myself for being a weak-minded idiot. I said as much to my son Michael, who was oiling his cricket bat, which he had laid down on the worktop in the kitchen, thus impeding my attempts to get supper.

"As soon as the words were out of my mouth I knew it was a stupid thing to have done," I said, reaching past him to get the corn flour out of a cupboard. "Darling, do you *have* to do that here?"

"I didn't think you'd want me getting oil all over the dining table," he said defensively, "and I've got to lay it down flat. Anyway, you surely won't have to do *that* much, will you? Surely, all those excellent women who hang around the deanery because of Francis will do the actual work. You'll only have to help poor old Joan organize things."

"It never works out like that," I said, remembering other times when I'd got myself involved in someone else's fundraising. "There's always a muddle, no one knows who's responsible for what, so guess who ends up doing the whole thing single-handed."

"I'm sure it's a very good cause," Michael said provocatively.

"The good cause is trying to rescue that poor woman from the ill temper of her dreadful husband," I said with some asperity. "It's not Culminster Cathedral's roof I'm worried about, it's Joan Beaumont's sanity!"

"Oh well, you managed the Red Cross auction okay," Michael said.

"Yes, but that was only a little affair—this'll be on a much larger scale and lots more people involved, not to mention horrible Francis breathing down one's neck! Oh, bother! This parsley sauce is developing lumps—hand me that whisk, will you."

Tuesday was a lovely day, warm and sunny but with a pleasant breeze, the sort of early English summer's day when the countryside looks so spectacularly lovely that you wonder why anyone would ever want to go abroad—until it's followed next day by a biting wind and torrential rain. Culminster Cathedral close, though small, is really beautiful, with honey-colored Georgian houses, some already festooned with great loops of mauve wisteria, set back from the cobbled road beyond close-cut grass verges. The deanery is large and imposing, three stories high and topped with a classical pediment. I wondered what on earth they used all that *space* for, since even Francis wouldn't have living-in servants to occupy those attics. I parked rather nervously in the small carriage sweep in front of the house and made my way up the short flight of steps to the heavy front door, with its lovely shell-shaped fanlight. Fortunately, there was a doorbell, since no ordinary human being would be capable of using the great brass knocker.

Joan herself answered the door. She was wearing an

afternoon dress of some sort of silky material with a paisley design in maroon and navy tied with a large bow at the neck, and looking exactly like a clergy wife in a play.

"Oh, Sheila," she said, "how good of you ..."

She seemed even more flustered on her own home ground than she had been at the assembly rooms, presumably because of the immediate presence of Francis.

"We always have tea in the drawing room on Tuesdays when Francis is at home," she said and led the way up the elegant curving staircase to the drawing room, which looked out over the close to the cathedral beyond. It was a handsome room, splendidly decorated, and no money had been spared to achieve an effect of taste and distinction. The furniture was antique (mostly Joan's, I believe) and beautifully kept, the carpets and curtains (obviously expensive) were just slightly faded so there was no jarring note of newness, and the pictures on the walls were mostly portraits or eighteenth-century oil paintings of classical landscapes. It was a lovely room, but all just a little too perfect for comfort. One couldn't have *lived* in it—well, *I* couldn't, and I had the feeling that Joan wasn't really happy in these formal surroundings. Francis, though, obviously saw them as a suitable background to his personality and position.

I became aware that the room had an occupant. Slumped in one of the chintz-covered armchairs was a young woman. She was large and rather lumpish, her appearance not helped by an unflattering tweed skirt with a cream-colored silk blouse already coming untucked from the waistband. Her dark hair was pulled back behind her ears with a couple of hair grips and she wore no makeup.

"You remember Mary," Joan said.

"Of course I do," I said, moving over toward her.

"Though I haven't seen you and Adrian for ages." I held out my hand and she rose awkwardly from her chair to shake it and then stood there uncertainly, seeming not to know what to do next. Feeling a faint flicker of sympathy for Francis, saddled with a terminally shy wife and an unprepossessing daughter, I sat down in the chair next to hers.

"And how's the library work going?" I asked.

She sat back heavily in the chair again and said, "Oh, it's all right."

There was a pause and then I went on rather desperately, "Are you still at Culminster Public Library?"

She nodded. "Yes," she said.

I always find it so difficult when people put a stopper on any conversational opening, like someone biting off a thread, and was just casting around for some other innocuous topic when the door opened and Francis came in. There are certain people who, on entering a room, seem to diminish everyone already in it. Francis is like that. It's not just his physical presence, though he is tall and well built and, I suppose, rather handsome. I've never been quite sure exactly what the word *charismatic* means, but I have a suspicion that it might well be used to describe Francis.

"Sheila!" he said, advancing toward me, hand outstretched. "How very good of you to come!"

His voice, although not as beautiful as David's nor as finely tuned, had the same deep timbre and resonance, which he used to great effect in cathedral services.

"It's nice to be here," I said conventionally.

"Splendid, splendid. Tea, I think. Joan, perhaps you would be good enough to ring for Mrs. Fletcher."

Joan took up her position by the table ladened with fine china and delicious-looking food (tiny sandwiches, scones and three sorts of cake) and Mrs. Fletcher, a robust little woman in a flowered apron, brought in a great silver teapot and hot-water jug. Also on the tray was a medicine glass, half full of a white, milky liquid that she passed to Francis.

"Poor Francis suffers dreadfully from indigestion," Joan

said, following my gaze. "The doctor says he has to take this special mixture before every meal."

Her earnest tone invested this small medical chore with an almost ritual significance.

Francis drained the glass and replaced it on the tray.

"Mary," he said, casting a stern look in his daughter's direction, "please assist your mother."

Mary got to her feet and passed cups and plates, proffering sandwiches and cake with her usual lack of manual dexterity.

"I was delighted," Francis said, dropping several lumps of sugar into his tea and stirring it with a finely engraved silver teaspoon, "to learn from Joan that you are to help us with our auction. I heard from Anthea what a success you made of the one at Taviscombe. In fact," he went on, "it would probably be better if you took over the whole thing from Joan, who would, I am sure, be the first to admit that she is not particularly gifted in that direction."

This was said coldly and with no mitigating smile. I looked at Joan, who had flushed, but who said earnestly, "It's quite true, Sheila, I'm really hopeless at organizing things—even after all these years!"

"I'm sure that's not so!" I exclaimed, not because I believed it, but because I couldn't bear to see Francis putting down his wife in this way. "Anyway, I couldn't possibly take over such a big event officially. I mean, I haven't any real connection with the cathedral—I'm not even a Friend, hardly even a casual acquaintance!"

Francis gave a little wintry smile in recognition of what he perceived to be a joke and said, "I hardly think that is relevant. You live in the diocese, after all."

"Oh yes," I said. "But think how many splendid ladies here in Culminster would be offended if someone from outside came and took over. Think of the umbrage that would be taken! No, Francis, I'll be delighted to give Joan any help I can, but it must still be seen to be her show."

Francis regarded me coolly. Obviously, he was not used to having his wishes set aside. After a moment he must have decided that, since he'd get my services anyway, he'd overlook this insubordination.

"As you wish, Sheila," he said. "We will be grateful for any assistance you can give. It will be a highly prestigious event. We have already received offers of many important pieces—furniture, pictures, jewelry and so forth. Sir Edward Clifford has promised us a very fine armoire, French, I believe, and Lady Felicity Gibbon is sending, among other things, a valuable diamond brooch that belonged to her grandmother."

"Have you got an auctioneer yet?" I asked.

"No," Joan said. "Well, there was an idea that Colonel Whipple *might* do it, but he's in hospital with his hip so we're in a bit of a fix ..." She looked at her husband and her voice trailed away.

"Only I've just had an idea," I went on. "We might persuade James Benson. You know he used to be at Sotheby's before he retired. And, *if* he did agree, we could make it like one of their evening auctions—evening dress, perhaps, but certainly formal, with glasses of wine and so forth."

I could see the idea appealed to Francis—he obviously fancied himself at the center of a rather grand social occasion.

"And if people are all dressed up," I said, "they're much more likely to spend a lot of money!"

Francis gave a nod of approval. "An excellent idea, Sheila. But will you be able to persuade Mr. Benson to do this for us?"

"Oh yes. He's an absolute poppet," I said, deliberately using a phrase I knew would irritate Francis, "and he was a great friend of Peter."

"A very useful contact," Francis said.

"An old friend," I said firmly.

"An evening occasion," Francis went on, ignoring my interruption, "yes, I think that would be very suitable."

I wondered if Francis was planning to appear in that splendid anachronism, clerical evening dress, but decided that was too much to hope for.

"Very suitable," he continued. "I am sure the bishop will be delighted that we have chosen such an appropriate and dignified way of conducting the affair."

We're very lucky that our suffragen bishop isn't one of those happy-clappy, evangelistic, pop churchmen (Francis certainly wouldn't have been a suitable dean for one of them), but on the other hand he's certainly not the snob that Francis's remark suggested.

"Oh, I don't think he minds a bit of informality," I said, more to annoy Francis than from any particular knowledge of the bishop's views. "He certainly seemed to be having a really jolly time at the Grand Pig Roast and Disco they had at Holford Treble last year in aid of their organ fund."

"A bishop," Francis said condescendingly, "would naturally feel it incumbent upon himself to appear to be enjoying any function, however bizarre."

"You may be right," I said. "Bizarre certainly describes *that* particular occasion!"

Francis then questioned me closely about the more technical aspects of organizing the auction and, apparently satisfied that I was to be trusted with the logistics, he closed the subject and turned his attention to his daughter.

"And have you finished looking through the muniment room catalog I gave you, Mary?"

"Yes, Father."

"And do you think you will be capable of continuing it in the same fashion?"

"I think so, Father."

He turned to me.

"Mary is taking a Library Association course on specialist libraries so that she can take over the running of our muniment room."

"How interesting," I said. "Will you enjoy that?" I asked her. "I thought you liked the public library."

Mary looked at me stolidly.

"It was all right," she said.

"It was never really *suitable*," Francis interjected, "dealing with all sorts and conditions of people." I raised my eyebrows at this unchurchmanlike remark. "No, Mary will be much better off here in the cathedral."

And under her father's eye was the unspoken comment. He resumed his questioning and seemed dissatisfied with her replies.

"You really must concentrate more on this course, Mary. You need to spend more time in study and less time gallivanting about the countryside on horses."

"Oh, do you ride?" I asked, pleased to have some point of contact with the girl at last. "I keep meaning to have another go—I used to love it. But it's been several years now and I keep thinking about how *stiff* I would be if I tried again! Anyway, the stables I used to ride from in Taviscombe have changed hands and I'm not mad about the new people."

"If you'd like to ride," Mary said eagerly, "there are some very good stables at Holcombe, just a few miles away. I know the person who runs them—I could come with you and introduce you."

Her face lit up with enthusiasm and she suddenly seemed a different person.

"Well, yes," I said, not really wishing to commit myself, but unwilling to quench the enthusiasm I had obviously aroused, "yes, I'd like that. I'll get in touch with you," I temporized, "and fix a date."

A flicker of annoyance crossed Francis's face.

"Mary has a great deal of work to do at present, Sheila, and has very little time for distractions."

Perversely, this decided me to accept Mary's offer and I said, "I'm sure Mary's working very hard, so I don't expect one morning off will make a great deal of difference. Anyway, when Michael was doing his law finals I insisted on his having little breaks to keep him fresh." This ingenuous remark obviously didn't cut much ice with Francis, but since he needed my help with the auction there wasn't much he could say.

Mary gave me a grateful smile and was just about to expatiate upon the excellence of the Holcombe stables when the door opened and a young man came in.

I hadn't seen Adrian for some years but he had hardly changed. From a tall, bespectacled, anxious boy he had grown into a tall, bespectacled, anxious young man. He had his father's build and coloring, even to some extent his good looks, but he also had his mother's timidity and her sad brown eyes.

"Ah, Adrian," Francis said. "You know Mrs. Malory, of course."

"Yes, indeed, how nice to see you again." His voice was Joan's voice, subdued and hesitant.

"It's nice to see you, Adrian. I was saying to Mary it's been such a long time ... but you haven't changed a bit."

Mary did not greet her brother in any way, but Joan began to pour a cup of tea when Francis stopped her.

"Adrian hasn't time for tea. He is here to come with me to see the treasurer before the chapter meeting this evening. You will excuse us, I am sure, Sheila. Cathedral business is always with us. It has been a great pleasure to see you again."

He rose and, with Adrian trailing in his wake, took his departure.

The door closed behind him, leaving an almost palpable feeling of relief and relaxation. Mary got to her feet and passed me a plate. "Do have a piece of Mrs. Fletcher's walnut cake, it's very good."

"And what about another cup of tea?" Joan said, pouring fresh water into the pot. "It's still nice and hot."

# 4

I hadn't heard anything from David for a couple of weeks and I was beginning to get worried.

"Do you think I ought to phone him?" I asked Michael. "Oh, don't hassle the poor man," Michael said. "He'll phone *you* if there's any news."

Michael is very fond of David but is of the opinion that I fuss too much about other people's affairs.

"I suppose so," I said doubtfully. "But I can't help being a little concerned. I mean, I know he had to see the bank round about now ..."

Michael stooped to unfasten the grass bag from the mower. "All the more reason for not badgering him—if it's all right he'll phone you; if it isn't he'll want to be left alone to brood a bit. Do you want this lot of clippings on the compost heap or put around the roses for mulch, like last time?"

"Oh, compost heap, I think. I'm sure putting it round the roses encouraged that wretched mildew. I expect you're right about David, but it's very frustrating not knowing what's going on."

"The trouble with you, Ma," Michael said, "is you're like the Elephant's Child, too full of satiable curiosity—and you know what happened to him!"

That evening I did ring but there was no reply, just the answerphone ("The last economy an actor makes, dear, is his answerphone") and David's voice saying: "If you want to leave a message for me or for Julian Yates, please speak after the silly little noise." But I didn't leave a message.

"It's so *desperate* for him, poor love," I said to my friend Rosemary when she came to lunch the next day (well, not proper lunch, just a piece of quiche and a tomato salad). "It's such a fabulous chance—it would be simply awful if he couldn't hang on until later this year."

Rosemary is fond of David, too, although perhaps less patient with him than I am. She finds it incredible that someone who made so much money in the days of his success should be so hard up now, but then Rosemary is married to a really good accountant.

"It does seem a bit hard," she said, "that Francis won't help. He must be filthy rich, but that's utterly typical of him. He always was a cold fish. Do you remember when Felicity Bradshaw was absolutely *mad* about him (and you must admit he was very good looking) and he strung her along because the family was rather grand—though poor as church mice— until Joan came along and *her* father was a bishop (so useful for him) and her mother had left her all that money, and he dropped Felicity just like that!"

"Goodness, yes!" I exclaimed. "I'd forgotten. And Felicity was really rather gorgeous, wasn't she, while Joan—well! Whatever happened to Felicity, anyway?"

"I think she went to Kenya, or was it Nigeria? With some man, an archaeologist or anthropologist—something like that."

"How extraordinary. Do have some more salad."

"Yes, please. Is this your own basil?"

"Yes. It's most peculiar, it's never germinated properly before, but this year it's simply taken over the greenhouse. Do remind me to give you a pot before you go."

"So how is Joan?" Rosemary asked. "I haven't seen her since that dismal garden party at the deanery in May, bitterly cold. That poor monseigneur, or whatever he was (I suppose that was Francis trying to be ecumenical, such a lot of nonsense) looked absolutely frozen, though *he* had lovely long robes on. But Joan looked pretty awful then. She had a terrible cold, I think, and should have been in bed, but I suppose Francis expected her to be there."

"What I can't bear," I said, "is the way he's always putting her down in public, treating her as if she was some sort of idiot. I can't think how she stands it!"

"Oh, she always was a doormat," Rosemary said briskly. "Do you remember her father? A dreadful man! He always resented the fact that Joan inherited her mother's money, of course. Anyway, he used her as a sort of unpaid secretary and slave for years. She always had to be at his beck and call, never went out anywhere. She only met Francis through some sort of church affair, when he was a curate."

"I'm surprised, really, that she was allowed to marry him."

"Oh, I think the bishop saw straight away that Francis was going places. He was very much a young man after his own heart—they were both very good with money—and I'm pretty sure he helped Francis up the ladder after he married Joan."

"It's all like something out of Trollope," I said. "I thought ecclesiastical circles were quite different nowadays."

"Well, it was nearly thirty years ago," Rosemary replied, "though I bet the money bit hasn't changed—got worse, probably. All this paying to go into cathedrals and gift shops everywhere! Anyway, what about Joan?"

"The same as ever, even more downtrodden if anything. If only she hadn't looked so pathetic I'd never have agreed to take on this auction thing."

"You really *have* let yourself in for something!" Rosemary exclaimed.

"I know," I said ruefully, "and it's going to be dire having Francis looking over my shoulder all the time to make sure I'm doing things properly! Still, if I can take the pressure off Joan ... I think she's having a difficult time with Mary, too, such a sullen girl—when Francis is about, anyway. And Adrian is a poor creature who just trails around after his father."

"Oh, I know! Jack has dealings with his firm from time to time and he says the boy really isn't very bright, dreadfully *slow*. He thinks that Francis simply wanted a son who was an accountant and poor Adrian had no choice in the matter! I know it took him ages to qualify."

"I suppose Francis hoped his children would be all forceful and ambitious, just like him, but they seem to have taken after Joan. Such a disappointment for him."

"Just as well, if you ask me," Rosemary said. "Think of the clashes of will and explosions if they had been!"

"I think they may just have an explosion with Mary," I said thoughtfully. "She's simply *seething* with resentment about her father—he's trying to make her work in the cathedral archive, or whatever it is, so she'll be even more under his thumb. He's even got her taking some special course and nagging her about it all the time. She really seemed on the edge of something last week."

The telephone rang and I got up to answer it.

"Oh, bother. I wish people wouldn't ring at lunchtime. Do help yourself to things."

It was David.

"Hallo, darling, sorry to disturb your lunch but I thought I might find you in."

"Oh, David, I'm so glad you rang, I was getting a bit worried about you."

"I would have phoned before but I've been exploring every avenue, as they say."

"Any luck?"

"No, not a thing. So I've decided to swallow my pride and ask Lydia."

"Oh, David!"

There was a heavy sigh at the end of the line. "I know, dear, but what else can I do? It's simply the Last Resort"—he spoke in capitals—"I can't think of anything else."

"Well," I said, "if she's any sort of feeling she certainly ought to help. Goodness knows what that flat in Highgate's worth now! And she's been in work for *years* now with that soap thing so she must be reasonably affluent. And you gave all that money to Eddy ..."

"Yes, well, we'll see. Lydia's always been a bit careful with money, but honestly, if she won't help then that's that!"

"Will you write, or what?"

"I think I'll go and see her—the personal appeal, you know. I'll stay with Piers and Keith, they live in Camden Town, quite near, and they've got a spare room."

"I'll keep my fingers crossed. Do let me know what happens. Please."

"I will."

I told Rosemary what David had said.

"Oh dear," she said. "I wouldn't think he's got much hope there. I only met Lydia a couple of times, when David brought her down here, but I can't say I ever took to her. Selfish, I would say, and not a very satisfactory mother—look how badly that boy has turned out."

"Eddy? I don't know that that was entirely Lydia's fault. I think he got in with a bad set ..."

"Only because she was too taken up with her own affairs (and I mean that in every sense of the word!) to notice what he was up to."

"You may be right," I replied. "I've always thought she was something of a disaster in poor David's life. Still, if she *does* turn up trumps now, I'll willingly eat my words."

"Goodness, is that the time? I must dash. Jilly's taking the baby to the clinic this afternoon and I said I'd look after Delia, so I must pop into that toy shop in the Parade and get one of those bubble-blowing things to keep her amused."

I was waiting in the dry cleaners while they searched for Michael's cricket flannels when a voice behind me said, "Miss Sheila? How are you keeping?"

Taken aback by this outmoded form of address, I turned and found David and Francis's old nurse standing behind me. "Why, Nana," I exclaimed, "how nice to see you!"

"I thought it was you," she said with an air of triumph, "you always did have your hair untidy at the back."

The man suddenly appeared with the trousers and I paid for them and then waited while the old woman engaged in some complicated transaction about a pair of curtains to be collected for cleaning.

"Because I can't bring them in," she repeated, "they're from the dining room, heavy brocade. With fringes," she added, as if this increased their intractability.

When she turned away from the counter I said, "Do you feel like some tea? Let's go and have a cup at the Buttery, it's almost next door."

She murmured assent and I settled her at a table in the corner while I went up to the counter to get the tea.

"I brought us a couple of cream eclairs," I said, "I hope you like them. Well now, how are you getting on in that great big house all by yourself?"

She embarked on a catalog of complaints, about the difficulty of "keeping it all nice."

"But, Nana," I said, "you don't *have* to stay there, you know. David and Francis would be very happy to find you a nice bungalow or something."

The old woman's face set. "Mr. Beaumont, rest his soul, left that house to me as a sacred trust for as long as I live. It was in his will. His last will and testament," she added, "and that's the law."

"But he didn't mean you *had* to live there," I persisted, "only that you could if you wanted. So that you'd always have somewhere to live. But there's no reason why you shouldn't go somewhere more convenient—the boys will happily pay the rent for you. I'm sure they've told you that."

"Master Francis is always on at me." Her voice rose. "He

came again only last week, and brought some man with him—I don't know who it was—looking round the place, they were. I told Master Francis, his father wouldn't like him bringing strangers in, traipsing all over the house, up in the attics as well. What were they doing up there, I'd like to know."

She cut cautiously into her eclair with a fork. "I've told Master Francis, *and* I've told Master David—though he's a good boy, he was always my favorite, such a sweet nature, just like his dear father ..." Her voice trailed away.

"Look, Nana," I spoke urgently, trying to get through to her, "poor David's in trouble, he needs a lot of money rather quickly and if you'd move somewhere else they could sell the house and he could have his share. Nana, you *know* how fond you are of David, I'm sure you'd want to help him ..."

"It wouldn't be right." She shook her head obstinately. "Mr. Beaumont wrote it all down in his will. I'm sorry about Master David, but if he's in trouble he must just make a clean breast of it, go and own up—honesty's the best policy, that's what I always told them."

"But Nana, it's not *like* that ...."

"And Master Francis"—she wasn't listening to me—"I keep telling him there's a lot of things that need doing, the outside paintwork's a disgrace—that's the sea air, of course—and the side door doesn't fasten properly and that man who does the garden hasn't been for two weeks running now, it's like a jungle out the back ...."

I gave up trying to talk to her about David and sat there listening to her rambling on, miserably aware that this old woman held David's future in her hands and that there was nothing I could do to make her realize how desperate the situation was.

# 5

I hate defrosting the freezer. It's not just the actual defrosting I mind (especially since Rosemary showed me how to melt those awful solid chunks of ice with a hair drier), so much as the shameful reminders of my own inadequacy as a housekeeper. All those anonymous, unlabeled packages, encased in a film of ice, that could be anything. All those undated shepherd's pies and apple crumbles—"make two and freeze one," the magazines say and I do, knowing in my heart that they will sit around in the freezer until I throw them out, together with the half used bags of Mixed Oriental Vegetables and the bake-it-yourself garlic bread that now looks like something that has been retrieved from an extra-slow-moving glacier. Why are other people so much more *organized*? My friend Anthea, for example. I once saw inside her freezer—everything labeled and dated, arranged in order of use—fantastic. Mind you, her children have all left home and she doesn't have any animals, still ...

I'd managed to get the freezer emptied and was wondering if two gelid, ice-burned pork chops that had somehow escaped from their wrapper would, if defrosted, be acceptable to our marauding foxes when the telephone rang. Irritated, I got up stiffly from where I'd been crouching on the kitchen floor and went into the hall to answer it.

"Yes, hello," I said brusquely.

A female voice I didn't immediately recognize said tentatively, "I'm sorry, is this a bad time?"

"No," I recovered myself, "not at all ..."

"This is Mary, Mary Beaumont." She stopped, apparently unable to go any further.

"Yes," I said encouragingly.

"Well, you did say—that day last week—that you *might* like to go riding, and I thought ..."

"Yes?"

"I thought perhaps you'd like me to fix up something with my friend at the stables at Holcombe."

"Ah." I opened my mouth to find some excuse.

"I told her all about you," Mary broke in eagerly, "and she's got a couple of very quiet horses—I mean, since you haven't ridden for a while."

In the face of such eagerness I knew I couldn't back down. "Well, yes, that's very kind of you, Mary," I said, trying to force some sort of enthusiasm into my voice. "When did you have in mind?"

"Next week, if that's okay with you. If you could let me know when, I'd try to arrange a free morning so I could come with you and introduce you to Fay."

"That would be lovely. Would Monday or Tuesday be all right?"

"Monday morning, about eleven o'clock, would be best. My father ..." She broke off, and I realized that this expedition to the stables wouldn't have his approval and that at eleven o'clock on Monday morning he would be safely occupied elsewhere.

"Monday would be splendid," I said, feeling agreeably conspiratorial. "Shall I call for you at the deanery?"

"Yes, that will be quite all right."

"Good. I'll see you then. Oh, I almost forgot, can your friend lend me a hard hat? I don't expect I'll be able to find mine after all these years."

"Oh yes, I'm sure she can."

"That's lovely, then, I'll see you on Monday."

I put the phone down and went back into the kitchen. I'd forgotten to put a cloth in the bottom of the freezer and quite a lot of melted ice had spilled out onto the kitchen floor and a neat set of paw prints showed where Foss had walked (deliberately) in the water and then up onto the worktop and thence onto the cooker. Sighing heavily, I reached for the floorcloth.

Michael was unsympathetic when I told him my plans for Monday morning.

"It's your own fault," he said severely. "You should harden your heart. Just because someone looks pathetic or hard-done-by, you don't have to let yourself in for goodness knows what."

"Well, I thought that if I cultivated the poor girl, won her confidence, I might be able to encourage her to stand up for herself against Francis, so *she* won't end up like poor Joan."

"Interfering in other people's lives," Michael said, "is a mistake!" He took some papers out of his briefcase. "You know you always end up by regretting it."

"Not always!" I protested.

"Well, nearly always. I suppose you'll have to go for this ride now you've said you will, but for heaven's sake be careful, don't fall off the creature—dangerous things, horses—and break anything. I don't want you ending up in hospital."

"Well," I said, touched by this expression of filial concern, "I'll take care."

"If you land up in hospital, who is going to iron my shirts?" Michael, opening a copy of *Tolley's Tax Law*, ducked as I threw a cushion at his head.

I'd hoped for heavy rain on Monday morning so I'd have an excuse to cancel, but it was a lovely day, fine and sunny, not too hot to encourage the flies that I remembered as a tiresome adjunct to riding. My jodhpurs and hacking jacket had long since been sent to a jumble sale, but fortunately I found my jodhpur boots tucked away on the top of the wardrobe in the spare room and, with those and my thickest trousers and a polo-neck sweater, I felt reasonably well kitted out. Not that my first riding instructor, Captain Kowalczyk, would have thought so. He was a former Polish cavalry officer who had ended up in Taviscombe after the war and ran the local stables when I was a girl. He insisted that his pupils were as properly turned out as his horses and was a ferocious taskmaster, barking out instructions to the local Pony Club aspirants as if they were about to lead a cavalry charge against the Prussian uhlans. I always remember hearing him saying to my friend Alison, an exceptionally small and fragile child, "No, no, you hold the reins in your *left* hand—your right hand is your sword hand!" No, Captain Kowalczyk would not have approved of my appearance, but I hoped it would pass muster with Mary's friend Fay.

Fay was a tall handsome woman in her mid-forties, with a brisk friendly manner.

"Mary told me you'd ride at about ten stone, so I've saddled up Prudence for you. She's very quiet."

Slightly put out at Mary's all-too-accurate estimation of my weight, I looked nervously at Prudence, who seemed to be an exceptionally *tall* horse.

"I've got some sugar lumps for her," I said. "Is it all right to give her a few—just to introduce myself?"

"Sure." Fay smiled.

I held out my hand flat, in a placatory fashion, with a couple of sugar lumps lying on the palm. Prudence vacuumed them up in one go, leaving a smear of greenish froth, and allowed me to pat her nose. She then drew back her lips in what I took to be a sneer and blew gently down her nostrils.

"Right, then," Fay said. "I thought you'd like to go a few

times around the tanbark just to get the feel of things again, and then Mary will take you out over the hill."

She gave me one of those new helmet things that people wear nowadays which I put on and led Prudence over to the mounting block. I managed to heave myself into the saddle and pick up the reins correctly.

"Oh dear," I said, "it's been a long time ..."

"Oh, you never forget," Mary said encouragingly.

And it was true. After a few circuits of the indoor ring I found that I was rising to the trot and sitting down in the saddle for the canter in the old familiar way.

"Okay?" Mary asked. "Shall we venture out?"

In her riding clothes (very neat and well turned out) and with the air of natural authority that comes with doing something you do well, Mary was a different person. She led the way along the (mercifully quiet) road and up a wide track into the hills behind Holcombe. She was a good teacher, too, tactfully and unobtrusively correcting my faults and making me feel that I was really doing rather well.

"Mary," I said impulsively as we stopped at the top of the hill to look at the magnificent view out over the Quantocks, "this is what you *should* be doing, not working in a library!" She gave a bitter little laugh.

"It's what I want to do more than anything in the world, but Father ... I've tried and tried to talk to him, Mother's tried too, but he won't hear of it, you can imagine! And he gets so angry."

"But Mary, you're, what are you? Twenty-three? Why don't you just go! What's to stop you?"

"I can't. He'd take it out on Mother, you know what he's like. Her life's wretched enough as it is—he'd go on and on! I'm sorry, Mrs. Malory, I shouldn't be talking to you like this..."

"Please call me Sheila and yes, I know what your father's like, I grew up with him. I know how—difficult—he can be, and I'm so very sorry for your mother. But you should be able to live your own life."

Prudence pulled at the reins and put her head down to crop the grass.

"Fay would like me to work at the stables—she's a wonderful person, well, you saw. It would be everything I've ever dreamed about. And now," her face darkened, "now I've got to work in the cathedral *with* him. He'll be around all the time, criticizing like he always does. Nothing is ever right for him. Adrian has had it for years, not that he seems to mind as much as I do. I think Father broke his spirit a long time ago, when he was a child. Poor Adrian, it's too late for him ..."

"Oh, Mary," I exclaimed, "I do wish there was something I could do!"

"There's nothing anyone can do," she said fiercely, "we're all helpless against him. All I can do is escape whenever I can, like today. Come on, let's make the most of it. There's a really good track along the top, no rabbit holes, quite safe for a gallop."

She touched her horse with her heels and was off. Prudence, suddenly aware of the loss of her equine companion, raised her head and moved forward. I shortened the reins and we galloped after the fast retreating figure, in flight, I felt, from the unhappy reality of her life.

The next day I was fine, full of plans for riding again, but the following day I was very stiff indeed.

"Oh God," I groaned as I tried, with some difficulty, to put dishes of food down for Tris and Tess. "Never again!"

"I thought you were planning to spend every spare moment in the saddle," Michael said, retrieving a slice of bread that had just shot out from the toaster. "A right little Annie Oakley."

"Yes, well, that was yesterday." I eased myself into a chair and sipped my coffee.

"Shouldn't you get straight back onto the horse again, or something?"

"Never. Never again."

"It seems a shame to give up just when you've started again," he said provocatively. "Anyway, won't Mary expect you to go on?"

I groaned. "You're probably right. It's a tragedy about that girl. Goodness, Francis has a lot to answer for! Think of the lives he's made miserable!"

"Not what you'd call a practicing Christian," Michael said. "Talking of which, any word from David?"

"No. He was going to try Lydia—I told you. I have a horrible feeling *that* was no good. I'm sure he'd have rung to tell me if it was good news." I got gingerly to my feet. "Perhaps if I soaked for ages in a hot bath I might eventually regain the use of my limbs again ..."

I heard nothing from David all that week, then on the Saturday he rang in the evening.

"David! How did it go with Lydia?"

"No luck, I'm afraid. Very sympathetic, of course, would have been only too *delighted* last year, but she's just gone and bought a farmhouse. In the Dordogne. And, of course," his voice rose in a perfect imitation of Lydia's plaintive tones, "you know how that simply *eats* money!"

"Oh, David, how unfair! She's got two homes and you're about to lose your one and only!"

"Well, dear, if it hadn't been that it would have been something else, I expect. Darling Lydia has never been exactly openhanded. I suppose I was a fool to expect any help from her."

There was a short silence while we both considered this palpable truth, then I said, "So what now?"

"I honestly don't know." He paused for a moment and then said, "Actually, Sheila, I wanted to ask you a favor."

"Of course, what is it?"

"Could I come and stay with you for a bit? You see, I told my bank I was going away for a while to try and raise the money—they've been really very patient, I must say, but there are limits ... I'm expecting them to get in touch any day now to see how I got on and, if I'm not there, unavailable (I'll tell Julian not to answer the phone, just leave the answerphone on), then they may think I'm still negotiating some sort of loan and give me a bit longer. I know I'm only buying time, but you never know, something may turn up."

"You know we'd love to have you. Come tomorrow."

"Bless you, dear, that would be marvelous. And, to be honest, I shall be glad to leave the house and everything. It's so dreadfully depressing to look around and think I may have to lose it all."

"Oh, David, I do understand. Look, get that twelve-something train, you change at Birmingham, and I'll meet you at Taunton. Okay?"

I put the phone down thoughtfully. Lydia had been David's last hope. I couldn't think, now, of any possible solution to the problem. Still, if a few days with us helped to take David's mind off the now inevitable loss of his beloved house and the destruction of his prospects, then we must do all we could to make his stay agreeable. I was sure his old friends would rally around—I must phone Rosemary—and try to arrange a few diversions for him. I went upstairs to make up the spare bed and turned my mind to the problems of catering.

# 6

David seemed quite cheerful when I met him at the station, but then I suppose being an actor is very useful when you want to conceal your real feelings.

"It always feels most *peculiar* to be back in dear old Taviscombe," he said as we drove through the outskirts of the town. "Do you think we could drive past the house? I'd like to have a look at it again."

I turned the car up West Hill and parked a little way away.

"Not right outside, dear, otherwise Nana might see us—she's still quite beady-eyed, I'm sure. I suppose I must go and visit her sometime, but, to be honest, I don't feel I could cope at the moment. When I *think* of all the money tied up in that place!"

Certainly it was a fine old house, large and imposing, built of the local red sandstone and surrounded by substantial grounds.

"You could get half a dozen bungalows in there," David remarked moodily. "Think of all that lovely *cash*."

"I think we'd better go," I said, "before you get all broody."

David is not an animal person himself, but being a sensitive soul he understands and is tolerant of animal worship in others, so he was not put out by the rapturous greeting the dogs gave him (barking and jumping up) and the signal honor bestowed on him by Foss, who curled up in his lap (covering him with cat hairs) the moment he sat down.

"I'm sorry, David," I said apologetically, "put him down if he's a nuisance."

"No, he's all right," David said, stroking the soft fur absently. "I can see, in a way, that animals might be quite a comfort. Undemanding."

I gave a snort of laughter. "That remark could only come from someone who never owned an animal!"

"Oh, we did have a dog when we were boys—some sort of terrier. We were supposed to look after it, to teach us responsibility or something, feed it and brush it, take it for walks, that kind of thing. When it was his turn, Francis, needless to say, was always busy with something else, so it was always left to me. It bit Francis once. It was a nice little thing..."

The days passed. We did nothing very much, went for drives to places we both remembered, seeing old friends, and David seemed reasonably happy. Some days he would go off on his own, wandering around the town, revisiting old haunts, walking by the sea.

"I must say," he said one afternoon, when he came back after one such expedition, "they've done their best to destroy the town. All those revolting cheapjack shops and racks of clothing outside—awful!"

"Yes," I replied sadly, "when you think what it used to be like. It's the council's fault—all those local shopkeepers being greedy, trying to make money out of the visitors and not considering the residents. There's simply nowhere to park now—fifty pence for an hour, if you can believe it—and no proper shops anymore, only horrible gift shops and cafés, the one and only fishmonger closed down last year. We mostly do our shopping in Taunton now."

At the back of my mind was the thought that if the worse

came to the worst and David lost his little house in Stratford, he might come back to Taviscombe. I was sure he couldn't bear to stay on in Stratford in some miserable lodgings. I didn't mention his troubles and neither did he, until Friday morning at breakfast he said, "I suppose I ought to telephone Julian and see if there have been any messages. I didn't give him your number on purpose, because I simply wanted to get right away. But one can't bury one's head permanently in the sand. Tonight, perhaps, quite late, if you don't mind, after he gets back from the theater."

"Of course," I replied absently, turning the pages of the local paper, "any time you like. Good heavens!"

"What's the matter?"

"Nana's dead!"

"What! What do you mean?"

"Here, in the deaths column. 'Esme Yates'—that's Nana's name, isn't it? 'Of Wootton Lodge. Aged 85. Funeral next Monday at All Saints. 12:30.' "

I put the paper down and we sat staring at each other.

"I suppose Francis put the notice in the *Gazette*," I said.

David didn't say anything for a moment and then in a voice quite unlike his own he said, "Can I have another cup of coffee, please, Sheila?"

I poured one for him and he spooned sugar into it. Then he said, "I'd better try and get hold of Julian. I expect Francis left a message."

He went out into the hall, but returned in a moment.

"No luck, he must be out jogging."

"Sit down and finish your coffee," I said, "then you must ring Francis."

We were both silent for a while, trying to come to terms with what had happened and all its implications.

"I wonder what she died of," I said. "She looked perfectly healthy when I saw her in the dry cleaners. I told you. That day when I tried to talk to her about you."

"Yes." David wasn't really listening to me. He reached toward the sugar bowl and had already put two more spoonfuls into his coffee when I reached over and took it away from him.

"David! You've already put goodness knows how much sugar in that cup already! Here, I'll pour you another one—you can't possibly drink that!"

I got up and fetched another cup. "There! And you really ought not to fill it with sugar—so bad for you. Look, I'll put some sweeteners in and see if you can tell the difference."

David laughed. "You always were a bossy girl and you haven't got any better with age! Actually, it's Nana's fault I have a dreadfully sweet tooth—Francis, too. It's one of the few things we have in common. She always put masses of sugar in things, tea, coffee, Horlicks, and lots of sweet cakes and puddings. People did in those days. Actually, this coffee's quite okay—I can't tell the difference."

"Good," I said, "the beginning of a healthy lifestyle. Here, take this pack of sweeteners, I've got some more, and keep it in your pocket in case you want any when you're out."

"I still can't take it in," David said, "that Nana's gone and all my troubles could be over."

"It does seem like a miracle," I said, "the U.S. cavalry galloping to the rescue just in the nick of time."

"It's the blessed sense of relief—I'd really got to the end of my tether. I feel quite light-headed. We must go out for dinner this evening to celebrate! Oh dear," he gave a rueful grimace, "what an awful thing to say! Poor Nana! I shouldn't have said that."

"It is a blessing," I said, "perhaps even for her. She was getting very confused, you know, and I don't believe anything on earth would have got her away and into an old people's home where she could have been properly looked after. She'd just have gone on getting dottier and dottier and living in terrible squalor, like those cases you read about in the papers."

"Yes, I suppose so. Still, I was fond of the old dear, in a funny kind of way, and she was a link with the past—the last one, really, unless you count Francis, and I don't because all my memories of him are pretty beastly. Which reminds me, I'd better ring him now and get it over with. Actually, Sheila"—he hesitated and then went on—"would you mind very much if I asked him to come over here to talk about things—I do so loathe going to the deanery and seeing him surrounded by all the pomp and majesty of the church. I always feel it puts me at a disadvantage!"

"Yes, of course. Invite him to tea, if you like. Or dinner, if you'd rather."

"Tea, I think. Dinner would be much too much of an imposition on you."

He went out into the hall again and I busied myself putting cups and plates into the dishwasher and clearing the table.

"Tea tomorrow," David said, coming back into the kitchen, "if that's all right with you? And, yes, it was Francis who put the notice in the *Gazette*, and it was very irresponsible of me to go away and not leave a telephone number, and why didn't I get in touch with him the moment I arrived in Taviscombe? Oh yes, and he has several things it is imperative he discuss with you about the auction as soon as possible. I think that's everything."

"Oh dear," I said, "I'd hoped to avoid another session about that wretched auction—I had planned to leave tea all ready for you both and go out somewhere to avoid him. Oh well, never mind. Perhaps he'll be so involved with your affairs and the house and everything, he won't have time for me."

"You hope!" David laughed. "Now then, is there anything I can do?"

"No, you go and read the paper or something—oh no, I tell you what—could you pop out and get me some eggs? I've only got a couple left and if I make a sponge *and* a walnut cake I'll need some more. I shall have to make the scones tomorrow, of course, so they'll be fresh ..."

"Sheila," David said sternly, "you're not to go to all this trouble for Francis!"

"Oh, it's not for Francis," I replied, "well, not as such. It's for my own amour propre—I can't be seen to fall below the proper standard! I always have to do the same when Mrs. Dudley (you know, Rosemary's terrible old mother) descends on me."

"I *think* I know what you mean," David said doubtfully, "and it will be lovely to have all that delicious cake, but it seems an awful lot of work."

"Well, actually, I've got an absolute *pig* of a book to review about Trollope—the author hasn't a vestige of humor, so you can imagine how dire it is—and I'm frantically finding excuses for not getting down to it!"

Francis was in a very affable mood, presumably pleased at the prospect of getting his hands on the house at last.

"I thought we'd have tea first," I said, "and then you and David can have a chat on your own."

After I had been put through a rigorous examination about my progress with the auction preparations, and after Francis had suggested various alternative ways of doing what I had already done, he sat back expansively and proceeded to tell us how clever he had been in various ways. He always did this when the brothers were together and I was careful not to catch David's eye, since it was something we joked about.

"As I expect you know, the cathedral's income last year was derived from five separate sources: 33.6 percent from grants, 9.2 percent from trust funds, 21.4 percent from donations and alms-giving and 6.3 percent from bequests. However, it is not generally realized that the final 29.5 percent comes from investments and commerce, and that is where I flatter myself I have been able to make a major contribution. Furthermore, by cutting back on last year's expenditure of 10.4 percent on administration and PR I have made a substantial saving ..."

I could see that David had already switched off and was staring pensively out of the window.

Taking advantage of a brief pause in Francis's monologue, I said, "More tea for anyone? Cake?"

Francis passed me his cup and continued. "Since the annual expenditure is in excess of one million—our music alone accounts for 16 percent of that figure ..."

I passed him the sugar bowl and assumed what I hoped was an expression of intelligent interest while he went droning on.

Eventually I was able to put the tea things onto the trolley and retreat to the kitchen. As I put the remains of the cake into tins and gave the few remaining scones to the birds (they're never very nice the next day) I wondered how David and Francis were getting on. I did hope that David was standing up for himself, though, from what I had gathered about old Mr. Beaumont's will, now that Nana was dead, the house and any bit of money that remained was left jointly to the two of them and they both had to agree to every step that was taken. I hoped this would be enough to protect David's interests, since Francis was very devious and if there was any way he could get a bigger share he'd certainly try to do so.

The dogs, whom I had shut out of doors because of Francis, reminded me with insistent barking that it was their mealtime and so I let them in. Foss also stalked in, furious at having been excluded from his own domain, and jumped up onto the worktop, where he walked up and down, complaining bitterly that the dogs were being fed before him.

I was just cutting up some raw kidney (his favorite food) when Francis came into the kitchen. Casting a disapproving eye at Foss, he said, "I have to go now, Sheila. I shall be in touch with David again quite soon. I gather he will be with you for some days yet. Thank you for a delightful tea." He held out his hand. My hands were covered in blood from the kidney and, flustered, I rinsed them at the sink, dried them hastily and imperfectly and shook the proffered hand. As usual, I felt Francis's disapproval washing over me.

"Good-bye, Francis," I said, placatingly, trying to retrieve some sort of credibility, "I'll certainly get in touch with Canon Bywater as you suggested."

He gave me a cold smile, his glance taking in the untidy kitchen, the dogs pushing their empty bowls hopefully around the floor and Foss, who had hooked a large piece of kidney off the cutting board into the sink, where he was crouched, chewing it ferociously with his head on one side.

"Good-bye, Sheila. It has been most pleasant."

"Give my love to Joan," I said, shepherding him into the hall, "and to Mary, too."

I closed the front door behind him and leaned against it, breathing a sigh of relief, then I went into the sitting room to see how David had fared.

"Well! He really outdid himself today—those dreadfully boring figures and banging on about how clever he'd been in getting in all that money and what the bishop said ..."

I became aware that David was sitting hunched up on the sofa looking miserable. I went over and sat down beside him and said gently, "David, what's the matter? What's happened?"

He looked at me sadly.

"Isn't it funny," he said, "just when you think things are going well at last, just when you think your troubles are really over, just when you've pasted a great big grin on your face, Fate comes along and kicks you in the teeth."

"David, what on earth are you talking about?"

He gave a weary little smile. "Francis doesn't want to sell the house. I'm right back where I started."

# 7

I stared at him in amazement.

"What do you mean, doesn't want to sell?" I asked. "I thought he was frightfully keen."

"Not anymore. He says the housing market's depressed and we wouldn't get a good price. He says we must hang on until things improve."

David was so depressed he didn't even bother to mimic Francis's magisterial tones. "He says we'd lose thousands of pounds."

"That's as may be," I replied, "but he knows what your situation is, how badly you need the money!"

"You know Francis," David said with an attempt at lightness, "always ready to consider his own needs before anyone else's."

"What about that man who wanted to turn it into a nursing home?" I demanded. "I thought he was prepared to pay a decent price."

"I asked about him—apparently he found somewhere else.

I'm not surprised, really, there are quite a few suitable houses on West Hill."

"Well then, what about some builder who could put up bungalows and starter homes or whatever in the grounds?"

"I asked about that too. Apparently the building trade's in a bad way and they're getting a bit sticky about planning permission. Oh, he had an answer for everything!"

We sat in gloomy silence for a while, then I said, "And there's no way you can go ahead on your own?"

"No way."

"Wouldn't the bank take your share as security or something?" I asked. "I mean, now that you actually *possess* it, now that Nana's dead."

"Not really," David said. "They've been quite good really, waiting so long. I don't think the *promise* of selling *sometime* would cut much ice with them now. I think they'd have to see the house actually on the market before they'd agree to hold off for a bit."

"There must be *something*," I said. "We'll ask Michael, when he comes home, if he can find some sort of legal loophole."

But Michael, when David explained the trust to him, was not hopeful.

"It's what we in the profession call a melamine job," he said.

"A what?"

"Unbreakable. I honestly don't see any way out of it. Your only hope is to try and persuade Francis to change his mind."

David sighed. "Well, you know how impossible *that* is!"

"Is there no sort of pressure you could exert over him?" I asked hopefully.

"I suppose you could threaten a sit-in in his cathedral," Michael suggested.

"He'd only have me thrown out by the vergers," David said.

"Actually," I said, "you *could* try a bit of subtle blackmail. I mean, you could let him know that you'd be telling people—influential people—just how badly he's behaved toward you. I mean, as dean he is supposed to be a practicing Christian! His brother's keeper—lit. and fig."

"I don't think I know any influential people," David said.

"Of course you do," I said, "and I'm really tapped into the network down here. My friend Anthea, for instance, knows the bishop quite well and there's nothing she likes more than spreading a bit of gossip."

"It might be worth a try," Michael said encouragingly. "Anyway, you've nothing to lose."

"It's not as though you *liked* Francis," I went on, "and even he, egotist that he is, must see that it wouldn't do his image any good for that sort of talk to get about."

"We-ell," David said doubtfully, "I suppose I might try. The trouble is, will I be able to carry it off? You *know* how I seize up when I try to talk to Francis!"

"We could work it out for you, like a script," Michael suggested, "then all you'd have to do would be to act the part of someone talking to his brother. Simple!"

"I tell you what," I said. "I promised Francis I'd go over to the deanery and look at some letters and things he's had about the auction, and I need to involve Joan a bit more so that the local ladies don't get too huffed about me doing too much. I'll suggest that you come with me—just to have a little chat."

"Oh, all right, then," David said resignedly. "As you say, I've nothing to lose."

Joan seemed pleased to see David. I'd forgotten that she had always liked him.

"It's been such a long time since we saw you," she said, her face quite lighting up with pleasure.

David was very sweet with her, making jolly conversation about nothing in particular so that she became quite relaxed and cheerful. Until Francis came in, that is. Then she reverted to her old uncertain self. It was really very sad to see the effect he had on her. David caught my eye and I could see that he, too, was struck by this.

"Well now," Francis said briskly to me, "I have most of the things I want you to see in my room in the cathedral, so if you come too, David, when Sheila and I have finished our business, she can come back here to have tea with Joan and you and I can have our little chat. I have to remain on call, as it were, in the cathedral, since I am expecting a visit sometime from the precentor—so tiresome, he couldn't give me an exact time, not a very efficient man, I fear." He turned to Joan. "Sheila will be about half an hour, so you can have tea at four o'clock."

Joan murmured assent and we obediently followed Francis out of the deanery and made our way through the close to the cathedral, Francis talking all the while about the restoration work, how much it was going to cost, the problems involved in finding such enormous sums, and, of course, how *he*, financial wizard that he was, was going to raise them. Culminster is not one of the great cathedrals of the southwest. The original Gothic building is marred by some rather heavy Victorian restoration work, but there are still many fine features. The arcading in the chancel is very beautiful and Pevsner praised the west front and maintained that the plate tracery in the Lady Chapel (foiled circles in groups of three—at least, I think that's what he said, I don't have a copy by me) may well have been executed by the same craftsmen who worked on the chapter stair at Wells.

We didn't enter the cathedral by the great west door but through a smaller one around at the side that I'd never noticed before. This brought us in halfway down the nave, already full of tourists. Some, milling about uncertainly, lifted their gaze from the printed booklets they were earnestly studying at the sound of Francis's voice ringing out as he continued his monologue as we made our way past the tombs of long-dead bishops. David and I had unconsciously lowered our voices as we entered the cathedral, but Francis, on his own home ground, saw no reason, I suppose, to speak in hushed tones, and I was reminded of Trollope's remark, in *The Small House at Allington*, about people who are accustomed to talking in churches.

We passed the door marked Vergers' Vestry, which has always intrigued me, and made our way into the south transept to the stairs that led up to the library and muniment room.

"I have a small office up here," Francis said as we made our way carefully up the narrow, winding stone stairs. "I find it convenient to work from here so I can keep an eye on things. A hands-on approach, I believe it is called nowadays." We emerged from the stairway into a large room with stone vaulting, with a massive oak door, leading through to the library, which stood open. In front of this door was a refectory table on which were piles of pamphlets and brochures, a beautifully arranged posy of flowers and a small cash box. Sitting at the table was a woman selling tickets for an exhibition in the library to a couple of tourists.

"You will find all the information about the documents in the cases and the chained Bible and so forth in *this* booklet," she was saying. Then, catching sight of me, she waved vigorously and I realized that it was someone I knew.

"Hello, Monica," I said, "fancy seeing you here!"

"Oh, I come in two afternoons a week—some of the Friends take it in turns. Good afternoon, Dean," she said, "quite a lot of people in today."

"Splendid, splendid," Francis said in his blandest ecclesiastical manner. "Keep up the good work, Miss—er—Mrs.—er ..." He strode on and we followed him.

"I'll see you when I come back," I said hurriedly to Monica as I passed, "we'll have a chat then."

Francis didn't go into the library but through a door on the other side of the room that bore the simple legend "Dean."

"Right, then, here we are," he said as we followed him in.

It was a largish room that also had stone walls and a vaulted ceiling. There was one large, arched window set in a massive stone frame, looking out onto the roof of the cloisters below. The whole tone of the room was medieval, ecclesiastical, monkish even, so it came as something of a shock to find that the main piece of furniture was a modern office desk on which reposed, as if on a shrine or altar, a very new, state-of-the-art computer. There were filing cabinets against the walls and a smaller desk, which held an electric kettle and a tray with cups and saucers, milk jug, sugar bowl and teapot, as well as several plates of sandwiches and cakes, neatly covered with cling-film. There was also the small glass containing Francis's indigestion mixture.

"Ah, good," Francis said, "Joan has brought our tea over. David and I will have ours here, Sheila," he explained carefully to me, as if to a not very bright child, "while we have our little chat, and you will go back to the deanery, where Joan awaits you. Now sit down, both of you, while I get out the papers I want Sheila to look at." He searched in the filing cabinet for a moment and then laid the relevant papers on the desk, pushing to one side a set of important-looking computer printouts.

"Now then ..."

One of the two telephones on his desk rang, the sudden, shrilling noise seeming strange and unsuitable, somehow, in such a place.

"Excuse me." Francis picked up the instrument. "Yes, yes, I quite understand, Archdeacon. I will see you later .... Yes. Good-bye. I'm sorry."

He replaced the receiver and spoke to David. "Cathedral business. I may conceivably have to go down to sort something out with the archdeacon later on, and then, as I told you, I must see the precentor—but I should be able to deal with them both quite quickly. We have plenty of time, since Evensong is, as you are aware, not until five-fifteen.

Now then," he turned to me, "here are the lists I mentioned of gifts promised, valuations where available—perhaps you could fill in the gaps there by consulting suitable authorities..." He broke off again as there was a tap at the door. "Yes, come in! What is it?"

Monica Woodward put her head around the door and said apologetically, "I'm *so* sorry to bother you, Dean, but the man from the printer is here about that new brochure—you said you wanted to have a word with him about those mistakes you found."

Francis made an exclamation of annoyance. "How tiresome, but, yes, I will see him now—if I don't I really hate to think what sort of muddle they will make. Excuse me."

He bustled out of the room. I made a face at David and said, "Goodness, how pompous! I suppose the world might conceivably stop turning on its axis if he wasn't in charge ..."

I got up and went to the desk to look at the papers Francis had got out for me. Some of them were mixed up with the computer printout and I had to sort them out. The roll of computer stuff seemed to be lists of shares, which I took to be part of Francis's restoration campaign until I saw that one sheet was headed "Francis E. Beaumont: Main Portfolio," so I supposed these were his own shares. I don't understand stocks and shares at all—they seem to have very peculiar names, some of them—and I haven't the faintest idea which are valuable and which are not or why they go up and down and cause such grief and anxiety to people like my friend Rosemary's husband, Jack. Still, judging from the list, Francis seemed to have a great many of them and it made me really furious to think that he had all these assets and had refused to lend a relatively small amount to his own brother when he knew that it was practically a matter of life and death.

Francis came back into the room and seemed rather irritated that I had picked up the lists from his desk.

"I hope you haven't disarranged any of the papers there," he said sternly. "I do like to keep absolute order in all things—

one thing out of place and the whole system is in jeopardy!"

I was aware of David stifling a giggle and I quickly apologized.

We went through the lists and I received my instructions.

"Yes, that's fine," I said, "I'll see to that tomorrow."

"Very well, then, Sheila." He looked at his watch. "Joan will be waiting for you."

Having unmistakably received my dismissal, I gathered up all the papers and put them into a shopping bag I had brought with me. I could see that Francis considered it an unworthy receptacle, but I'm really not the sort of person who feels comfortable carrying a briefcase.

"Now then," Francis said, "will you both be staying for Evensong?"

I looked inquiringly at David, who hesitated for a moment and then said, "Yes, I'd like to, if that's all right with you, Sheila?"

"Yes, that'll be fine. Will you come over to the deanery and collect me about five? Good-bye, Francis. I may see you later, then."

"Splendid, splendid," Francis said. "Now, David, if you would be kind enough to switch on that electric kettle on the desk beside you, we will have our tea."

I closed the door carefully behind me, encouraged by the almost benevolent tone in which Francis addressed his brother.

"Wasn't that David Beaumont?" Monica Woodward demanded. "The actor who used to be in that thing with the detective, on the television."

"Yes," I replied. "David's the dean's brother."

"*Really*! I never knew that! An actor! It seems unsuitable, somehow."

"Oh, I don't know," I said. "The church and the stage have much in common, and, after all, the theater had its origins in religious ritual."

"Oh, but that was in ancient times—pagan rites and so forth," she protested.

"Well, there were the miracle plays in the Middle Ages," I persisted, more for my own amusement than from any wish to convince her.

"But they were Roman Catholic," she countered, "and, anyway, television's *quite* different."

I laughed. "Well, you may be right." To change the subject I continued, "What pretty flowers." I leaned over to smell them. "Who did the arrangement?"

Monica looked gratified. "I did. I always like to keep fresh flowers up here, though of course I'm also on the rota for the proper flower arrangements in the cathedral itself. It's something I've always rather liked doing, so even when I'm not actually on duty here I try to pop in and see that they're nice and fresh. I always think there's nothing quite so depressing as dead flowers."

"They're lovely! Well, I must be getting on. I'm having tea with Mrs. Beaumont and I don't want to keep her waiting."

"Sheila!" A voice behind me made me turn around. It was Mary, who had just come out of the library. "Have you been to see Father?"

"Yes, I've just left him with your Uncle David and I'm on my way to have tea with your mother. Are you coming?"

"No, I'm working here now and I'm rather busy at the moment. When are you coming riding again?"

"Oh, very soon," I said evasively. "Next week, perhaps. I'll let you know."

"You did like the stables, didn't you?" she asked anxiously. "I thought Prudence suited you very well, but we could easily find you another horse if you'd rather."

"No, I was very happy with Prudence—most ladylike—and I thought the stables were splendid."

"And Fay? She's terrific, isn't she?"

"Terrific. I liked her very much. Look, I really did enjoy

myself, although I was dreadfully stiff afterward, though I expect that will get better. So I will give you a ring next week to fix up another ride. Now I must go or I'll be late."

I could see Monica Woodward was drinking in all the details of my acquaintance with the various members of the Beaumont family. She would doubtless be passing them on to the other Friends, especially those who resented my involvement with the auction, with suitably pointed comments.

"Good-bye, Monica," I said with my brightest smile, "keep up the good work!"

I made my way carefully down the worn treads of the stone stairs, clutching the heavy rope attached to the wall that served as a handrail, and walked slowly down the left-hand side of the nave so I would pass my favorite tomb. There are two effigies. One is of a knight, Richard of Molland, a Crusader with his legs crossed, but his little dog, instead of lying quietly and traditionally under his feet, is tucked comfortably under his knees. His wife, Elizabeth, robed and wimpled, lies beside him. I always wonder if she cared for animals too. I think not, since her expression—even though time has blunted her features—is not amiable.

The cathedral was emptier now, most of the visitors having made their way to the tearoom ("cream tea £2.50"), and the choir was rehearsing a setting of the Magnificat, their splendid voices soaring up until they seemed to be absorbed into the glorious stone arches and the vaulted roof.

> He hath put down the mighty from their seat: and
> hath exalted the humble and meek.
> He hath filled the hungry with good things: and the
> rich he hath sent empty away.

I wondered if Francis ever actually listened to the words of the service.

# 8

I looked up at the drawing-room window of the deanery as I crossed the close and, sure enough, there was Joan's worried face peering down. I waved and she quickly withdrew, presumably hurrying downstairs to open the door, which stood open for me when I mounted the steps. Joan was hovering anxiously in the hall.

"Is everything all right?" she asked.

"Yes," I replied in some surprise, "is there any reason why it shouldn't be?"

"No, of course not—well—it's just that Francis wasn't very pleased about David coming over, actually."

"Oh?"

"Well, he didn't say anything in so many *words*," Joan said, "but I could tell—he spoke very disparagingly about him and he's been dreadfully irritable all day ..."

"Well, he was perfectly civil to David—quite amiable, in fact, considering that they've never got on."

"No," Joan sighed, "*such* a pity! We hardly ever see him now, but in the old days I always found David so agreeable, such good company."

"Yes, bless him, he's very sweet—a thoroughly nice person."

The words "unlike his brother" hung in the air between us.

"Well, anyway," I went on, "at this moment, they're having tea together in a perfectly civilized fashion."

“Oh, tea!” Joan exclaimed, “do come up—it’s all ready.”

Tea was laid out as before in the drawing room, but without Francis’s restrictive presence it was a much cozier meal and Joan became positively animated. In fact she chatted away almost nonstop, as if all the casual conversation, the ordinary interchange of everyday life, had been denied to her for so long that she had to come out with it all at once. With me (and with David) she felt relaxed and safe and I caught a glimpse of the person she might have been if it hadn’t been for her formidable father and authoritarian husband. Very sad.

“I did enjoy my ride with Mary,” I said.

“Oh, she loves being at the stables,” Joan sighed. “If only... her friend Fay offered her a partnership, you know. I still have a little money of my own—a trust of some kind—and I’d have been very happy to lend her what she needed, but Francis ...”

“Oh well, I expect she manages to fit in a few rides at weekends and so forth.” I tried to turn the conversation to more cheerful topics. “How’s Adrian? I believe he’s doing very well.”

This mention of her son, however, was not a success. Joan’s face clouded.

“I’m really very worried about him. He’s never been very strong, a really nervy boy, if you know what I mean.”

Not surprising with Francis’s critical eye on him all the time.

“He’s so unhappy! He never wanted to be an accountant,”

Joan burst out. “He wanted to be a vet—he’s marvelous with animals—but Francis had made up his mind. It was such a difficult time—all those exams and Francis was so angry when Adrian didn’t pass, which made it worse, of course.”

Poor Adrian, no wonder he looked like a shadow.

“I’ve often wondered,” I said, “why Francis didn’t

become an accountant himself—he has such a flair for figures—or some sort of businessman. Why the church? Not that he hasn't done marvelously well, being a dean and everything, and great scope for his organizational abilities, but still ..."

"I think he always saw himself as a bishop," Joan said, "right from the beginning, even when he was a curate—I know my father thought so, too."

"You mean, he liked to think of himself as a prince of the church. What a pity," I said frivolously, "he isn't an RC, then he could have become a cardinal. Scarlet *would* have become him!"

"But if he'd been a Roman Catholic priest, he couldn't have married," Joan said and I realized I had gone too far in my flight of fancy for her to follow.

"I was only joking," I said and she laughed dutifully.

I changed the conversation to more mundane matters—the recipe for Mrs. Fletcher's chocolate cake, the proposed visit of the bishop to Bulgaria, the difficulty of finding elastic in any of the local shops—and soon we were quite cozy again.

At about a quarter to five I was just glancing at my watch and wondering about Evensong when the doorbell rang. Joan went down to answer it and came back with David.

"Oh good," I said. "I was just wondering when we ought to go along ..."

"If you don't mind, Sheila, I'd rather not go to Evensong." David's voice was strained and his face was stony.

"David! For heaven's sake, what's the matter?" I got up and went toward him. "What's happened?"

"After the totally unchristian way my loathsome brother behaved this afternoon," David said furiously, "it would be the worst kind of mockery to listen to him taking any sort of church service."

Joan, in the doorway, gave a little moan and he turned toward her and said, "I'm sorry, Joan, I don't want to upset you, but I have to say that I don't think I can ever bear to see Francis again."

I've never seen him so angry.

"But David," I repeated, "what's happened?"

"I asked him once more—no, I *begged* him—to reconsider selling the house. I told him how my entire life would be in ruins if we didn't. He absolutely refused to consider it."

"Oh, David!"

"Furthermore," he continued with considerable bitterness, "he then had the incredible *cheek* to lecture me about my choice of profession, my lifestyle, and what he chose to call my lack of thrift and failure to make provision for my old age!"

"Oh, David, I *am* sorry!" I said. "How despicable! I'm sorry, Joan, but I'm sure you know just how much all this means to David. His whole future depends on it."

"No," she faltered, "Francis never said ... he never discusses anything to do with money with me ... I'm so sorry, David."

"Well, I finally lost my temper," David said, "and told him all the things I've wanted to tell him all these years, got it all off my chest!"

"Goodness," I said, "how did he take that?"

"Oh, he stayed on his high horse, went on pontificating, the way he always has. You can never really get through to him, he simply can't believe he's in the wrong. In the end I was actually shouting at him!"

"Good heavens!" David's splendidly pitched actor's voice is always totally audible even when he is speaking quietly; shouting, he must have been audible all over the cathedral. "I bet Monica Woodward was drinking it all in!"

"Monica ... ?"

"The woman at the table, selling the tickets just outside the door."

"Oh dear," Joan said, looking stricken, "and she's the most terrible gossip—it'll be all over the place tomorrow!"

"Well," I said firmly, "Francis has only himself to blame.

You must admit he's behaved abominably. Come along, David, we'd better go. I presume Francis won't be back here before the service, but even so, I for one would prefer not to run into him."

"No," Joan replied, "he said something about seeing the precentor so he won't be coming back until after Evensong."

"Good," I said. "And you'd better tell him from me that he'll have to find someone else to arrange the auction for him because there's no way I'd have anything to do with it now!"

She protested, but only halfheartedly, and I felt rather mean leaving her to cope with things on her own, especially as Francis would be livid and take his ill temper out on her. But, as I said to David when we were driving back to Taviscombe, she was probably used to that by now.

David had recovered his usual equanimity by the time we got home, but he was very depressed.

"I simply can't think of any other way to raise the money," he said, "unless I go to the loan sharks."

"No way," I said. "We must just keep on thinking. There must be something. Anyway, try and put it out of your mind for one evening. Look, Michael will be back soon, let's all go out to dinner—there's a new place out at Toland, an old water mill or something, they say the food's very good. I'll try and book a table now."

It wasn't a very festive evening, although the food was very good and the atmosphere was agreeable, and we all tried very hard, but there were silences that had to be broken with determinedly cheerful remarks and even a really splendid white burgundy didn't promote the feeling of relaxed well-being that I had hoped for. It wasn't surprising, I suppose. Poor David really had come to the end of his tether; there seemed nothing else he could try.

I was up about six-thirty the next morning. Both the dogs are getting old now and I like to let them out into the garden as early as possible. I stood in the kitchen waiting, in my usual early-morning stupor, for the coffee to drip through the filter and idly watching Foss carefully inspecting every plant and shrub for traces of his old enemy, a black and white farm cat who pays us nightly visits. I was shaken out of my reverie by the telephone, ringing, it seemed, with particular insistency. It was Joan.

"Sheila? Is David there?"

"He's still in bed," I replied, bewildered by the unexpectedness of the call. "Do you want me to fetch him? What's the matter, what's happened?"

"It's Francis ..." I suddenly realized that she was crying. "He died in the night."

"Oh, Joan, I am sorry! What was it? I mean, how? Was it a heart attack?"

"We don't know, the doctor's not certain .... It's all been so awful. I'm so sorry to ring you at this hour, but I've been up all night ..."

"For goodness sake! That doesn't matter at all. I was up anyway. Can you tell me what happened?"

"Yes, well ..." There was a pause while I heard Joan blowing her nose and she continued more composedly. "He wasn't really himself when he got back from Evensong—vague almost, and *that's* not Francis, as you know. He went into his study and I didn't see him for a bit, because he doesn't like to be disturbed when he's working. About seven-thirty I tapped on the door and called out that dinner was ready, but he didn't reply. I waited a good fifteen minutes in case he was in the middle of something he wanted to finish, you know, and then I went into the study and found him ... The tears threatened to return but she went on. "He'd collapsed onto the floor, he must have fallen from his chair. I didn't know what to do, so I called for Mary and she said his pulse was very faint, but he was alive."

"Oh, Joan, how dreadful for you!"

"Mary phoned the doctor and he came round straight

away," Joan went on, wound up now and intent on telling her story. "Then the ambulance came and took Francis to the hospital—Mary and I went too. Dr. Marlow was very kind, he took us in his car. He said Francis was in a coma, whatever that means—I don't know much about such things. But, when we got to the hospital Francis was dead. Dead on arrival, is what they said. I suppose he died in the ambulance .... They were such nice men, the ambulance men, I'm sure they did everything they could ..."

"I'm so very sorry. It must have been a terrible time for you. I'm so glad you've got the children with you."

"Mary's been wonderful—I really don't know what I'd have done without her, she's been a tower of strength."

"And Adrian too, I'm sure."

"Adrian?" Joan's voice broke. "Oh Sheila, it was quite dreadful! He wasn't in for dinner so when all this happened just Mary and I were there. And then, when Dr. Marlow drove us back from the hospital, Adrian had just got in. I told him what had happened and—oh, I shall never forget it!—he broke down completely, sobbing, really hysterical, it was quite frightening. Thank goodness Dr. Marlow was there—he quietened him down and gave him some sort of sedative—he's still asleep."

"Poor Adrian!" I said. "I suppose it was the shock—he's always been very highly strung."

"Yes." Joan sounded subdued. "But it was so violent. I do hope ..."

She paused and I said as bracingly as I could, "Well, I'm sure Mary is a great comfort to you. I wonder," I went on tentatively, "did they say at the hospital what Francis died of?"

"No, they didn't seem sure. Dr. Marlow says that because it was a sudden death there'll have to be a postmortem. I really don't like the idea of that, and I know Francis would have been very angry, but he says it's the law and we have to."

"Oh dear, how distressing for you."

"Anyway," Joan said, "I thought I'd better tell David. Actually," she hesitated, "would you mind telling him—after yesterday, it's a bit embarrassing."

"Of course I will. I'm sure David will be very upset. He really isn't a quarrelsome sort of person—well, you know that—but Francis was being so difficult ..." I broke off, aware that I was speaking ill of the dead. "Look," I said, "would you like me to come over? Is there anything I can do?"

"Oh, Sheila, could you? It would be such a comfort. And, well, if David *would* care to come I'd like to see him. I do understand about yesterday—please tell him that."

"Thank you, Joan, I know that'll mean a lot to him. Right, then, we'll be over later this morning. Now, look, have you had anything to eat?"

"No, I ..."

"I thought not. You've got to have something or you'll be no use to anyone," I said briskly. "Go and make yourself some toast and a cup of coffee, and put some brandy in it!"

"Oh, I don't think I could do that. But I will make some breakfast. Mary will want something when she wakes up. Poor girl, she's still sleeping. She was absolutely exhausted, but I couldn't go to bed, it seemed wrong somehow."

"You go and get that coffee," I said, "and we'll see you later."

I didn't wake David, there seemed no point, time enough to tell him when he came down.

"Francis? Dead? Oh God, how awful! If only I'd kept my mouth shut one more time!" David was genuinely upset. "After all these years! Poor Joan, she must be in a state. How is she coping?"

"Reasonably well, considering, and Mary's apparently turned up trumps. Which is just as well, since Adrian's being a broken reed." I told David what Joan had told me about his collapse.

"Poor lad," David said sympathetically, "it must have

been absolute hell being Francis's son and Adrian always was a feeble creature."

"I told Joan I'd go over later this morning," I said, "and she said *if* you felt like going too, she'd be glad to see you."

"Ah," David grimaced, "to be absolutely honest, I *don't* want to—but if you think it would make Joan feel better, then of course I will."

I smiled at him affectionately. "If you could bear it, then I think she would be pleased—the family rallying round, as it were," I said.

We sat at the kitchen table, drinking coffee and not saying anything. After a while I said, "Well, now you really *will* be able to sell the house. I know it's not the way you would have wanted it to happen, but it really does seem that your troubles are over—I can't think of anything that could go wrong now."

"No," David said. "I wouldn't have wished Francis dead, in spite of everything, but, since it's happened, I'd be a hypocrite if I didn't admit to a feeling of relief. No, apart from the world coming to an end, or something over the top like that, I think it's going to be all right."

When we arrived at the deanery Joan was quite calm, though her eyes were still red and I felt she was holding onto her composure with difficulty. She was wearing a black dress—I suppose clergy wives need to have some sort of mourning by them for funereal occasions. She greeted David affectionately and he gave her a brotherly hug and sat beside her on the sofa listening attentively while she went over again the events of the night. After a while Mary came in.

"Oh, hello, Sheila, Uncle David, it was good of you to come."

The difference in her attitude and, indeed, her appearance was dramatic. The timid, sullen girl had gone, transformed into an assured, almost brisk young woman in a navy suit. Even her hair, today let loose from the restraining hair grips, seemed softer and more becoming.

"Mary, I'm so sorry," I said, taking her hand, "it must have been a dreadful night for you both. Now, is there anything practical we can do?"

"Not really, thank you all the same," she replied. "But until they've established the cause of death we can't do much about the formalities."

"The bishop has been so kind," Joan said. "Of course Mary rang up his chaplain first thing this morning. And the bishop rang me back straight away. He said that we must take all the time we want, looking about, you know."

"Looking about?" I echoed.

"For a house," Joan said.

"The deanery goes with the job," Mary said wryly. "Tied accommodation."

"Oh, goodness, how dreadful for you!" I exclaimed. "What will you do? Will you stay in Culminster?"

"I shall move in with Fay at the stables," Mary said. "It's what I've always wanted. And, most fortunately, there's a nice cottage for sale almost next door that Mother and Adrian can buy."

I was slightly taken aback by the briskness of her response, with her father so recently dead. I looked at Joan, wondering how she would take this management of her life, but she seemed perfectly happy to leave everything to Mary. I suppose she was so used to having no control over her own life that she would have been lost without someone to tell her what to do.

"And how's Adrian this morning?" I asked.

"Poor boy," Joan's face clouded with anxiety, "he's still in bed. This has really upset him—he's very shaken."

Mary gave a faint exclamation of impatience and I suddenly realized that, under that repressed exterior, there was something of her father. Certainly, although she didn't have his good looks, there was in this new Mary a kind of physical resemblance in the way she moved and in certain facial expressions. I wondered if Joan might be exchanging one sort of domination for another, though I was confident that Mary was a naturally kinder person than Francis.

Joan produced coffee and we sat around talking—more about Mary's plans for the stables and her new life, I noted, than about Francis's death. I thought how furious he would have been not to be the center of attention at such a time.

"Mother will need to make an offer for the cottage fairly soon," Mary was saying, "because I know there have been a few inquiries about it and it would be so perfect ..."

The phone rang and she got up to answer it.

"Well!" I said, instinctively using an equestrian metaphor after all the horsey talk there had been, "Mary does seem to have taken the reins into her own hands."

"Yes," Joan said, "she's been marvelous. I don't know how I'd have coped without her."

Once a doormat, I thought, and, catching David's eye and his faint smile, I saw that he felt the same.

"How will Adrian feel about moving out there?" I asked.

"Oh, I'm sure he'll think it's for the best," Joan said eagerly. "He can easily come into Culminster to work every day—it's quite a short drive—and I think the country air will do him good."

Mary came back into the room. Her face was expressionless but, from her demeanor, it was obvious that she had important news.

"That was the police," she said. "They say that Father died from morphine poisoning."

# 9

"But that's impossible!"

Joan's cry voiced the thoughts of us all.

"But surely ..." I began.

"But he wasn't taking anything—only his indigestion mixture, nothing else!" Joan said in some agitation. "I would have known if he was!"

"Well, the inspector is coming round to talk to us about it now," Mary said.

"The police! Oh no, Francis would hate that! And what will the bishop say?"

"Well," Mary said bluntly, "the bishop will just have to lump it."

Joan gave a faint cry of distress at this revolutionary statement and Mary continued more softly, "I'm sure he'll be very sympathetic, Mother, he's a nice man. Anyway, there's nothing we can do about it. It's in the hands of the police now."

"Perhaps we'd better go," I said. "We'll be in the way."

"No, *please* stay," Joan pleaded, and I could see that she would be grateful for the sort of buffer (against the masterfulness of her daughter as well as the intrusion of the police) that a sympathetic female friend of her own generation could provide.

"Perhaps there's been some mistake," Joan went on hopefully. "I mean, they may have got the results of the postmortem mixed up with someone else."

No one commented on this unlikely possibility and we sat in silence for a while, trying to take in this extraordinary turn of events.

Joan turned to her daughter.

"Did your father say anything to you about having seen a doctor?"

"No, but then he wouldn't, would he? The only conversation we had these days was about me not working hard enough at that stupid exam, or some other criticism." Mary's voice was harsh and I saw Joan shrink back at the tone.

"He only wanted what was best for you, dear," she said pleadingly. "He was so looking forward to you taking over the cathedral archive, and you know you liked working there."

Mary received this remark in a silence that was more eloquent than any reply.

The front doorbell rang and Mary went to answer it.

"This is Inspector Hosegood," she said, ushering him into the drawing room, "of the Culminster CID."

"*CID*!" Joan exclaimed.

"Nothing for you to worry about," the inspector said, "it's just that in—er—unusual circumstances like this we have to make inquiries. Just routine."

Inspector Hosegood looked more like a farmer than a detective. He was a large, burly man wearing a battered Barbour jacket, a checked shirt and corduroy trousers. He had a high color and his face had that weather-beaten look that comes from spending some time out of doors. His close-cropped fair hair was sprinkled with gray, his manner was relaxed and friendly and he spoke with a distinct West Country burr, which I found somehow comforting.

"Just a few routine inquiries," he repeated reassuringly.

"Yes ... Oh, please excuse me. This is my daughter Mary and this is my husband's brother, David Beaumont, and this is my friend Sheila Malory, who very kindly came over ..."

"Good morning." Inspector Hosegood gave a slight nod in the general direction of the company. "Now, Mrs. Beaumont, if we could have a few words?"

"Yes, of course ..."

"Take the inspector into the study, Mother," Mary suggested.

"Your father's study? Oh no, I couldn't do that! We'll go into the dining room."

I saw the inspector react to this.

"Would you like a cup of coffee, Inspector?" Mary asked. "Oh, dear, I should have offered ..."Joan said.

"That would be very nice, Miss Beaumont, thank you, if it's no trouble."

They all three went out of the room and David and I looked at each other.

"Morphine! Francis!" I exclaimed. "Surely there wasn't anything wrong with him? I mean, you have to be pretty ill to have morphine, don't you? You don't think ... it couldn't be *drugs*, could it?"

"Francis! Taking drugs! It couldn't be!" David said firmly. "Anyway, is morphine that sort of drug? Do you *take* it like that?"

"I don't know. One is so ignorant about things."

"Well, even if you can, I can't believe Francis would."

"No, I suppose not. It's all very peculiar. Poor Joan! Francis dying was upsetting enough, but if there are suspicious circumstances—isn't that what they call it?—then I hate to think how she'll cope."

"She won't have to. Mary's obviously determined to run the whole show. Would you have *believed*!"

"I know, isn't it extraordinary! A complete transformation! I'd never have thought it possible. When she was at the stables she was different, of course, but *this*! Perhaps she's always been like this inside and Francis's death has sort of *released* her."

"Just as well, in the circumstances. I have a feeling Joan is going to need all the help she can get in the next few weeks."

Mary came back into the room then so we couldn't pursue this fascinating line of thought anymore.

"He seems a pleasant man," I said, "the inspector. Not intimidating at all."

"Yes, very pleasant," Mary responded vaguely. "He says," she continued, "that there'll have to be an autopsy."

"Oh dear, how distressing for your mother," I said sympathetically.

"Yes. I wonder what they'll find?"

Joan came in. "The inspector's gone," she said. "He says he will be coming back to tell me what they find .... He was a nice man, he quite understood how difficult it is—the bishop and everything."

"Well now," I said. "Is there anything we can do? Otherwise we should really be getting back to Taviscombe."

"There is one thing, Sheila," Joan said. "I would like to go on with the auction. Will you help me? I know Francis would have wished us to."

"The auction?" I said in some surprise. "Why yes, if you want me to, of course I will."

"I'd have thought the last thing Joan would have wanted at a time like this would be that auction thing," David said as we drove back.

"Oh, I don't know," I replied. "One final thing she could do for Francis, perhaps. Actually, I've done most of the groundwork, it just needs a few final arrangements. Joan won't have to do much, just enough to make it look as if she's running the show."

"*Aren't* you efficient!"

"Years of hard-won experience! Oh dear, I wonder how she'll manage, though? After all these years being a doormat to Francis and putting up with his bad temper, do you think she feels free at last, her own person?"

"I doubt it. People like that are only really happy when they're being bullied by *someone*."

"I wonder," I said thoughtfully. "She may have hated him for all we know and be glad he's dead. There've been moments when I felt a sort of seething resentment under all that submissiveness. Anyway, do we ever really understand other people? Look at Mary and what an extraordinary transformation there was there!"

"Well, she's young and the young are more flexible than we are. I wonder if Joan really wants to live in that cottage Mary's got lined up for her. And what about Adrian?"

"Oh he's been so conditioned to obedience by his father," I said, "that I doubt if he has the ability to question anything anymore."

"You don't think he'll be all strong and positive now, like Mary."

"Hardly, since he seems to have gone completely to pieces—still in bed when we were there, Joan said. No help at all." I gingerly overtook a tractor with a large and unstable load of silage and continued, "I wonder what they'll find at the autopsy? I suppose they'll be able to tell when Francis took the morphine and what sort it was."

"I suppose so."

"If he wasn't taking it for some illness, I mean, if it wasn't prescribed by his doctor—and come to think of it, it can't have been, because Mary called their doctor right away and, if *he'd* prescribed it, he'd surely have said something then. No, if it wasn't prescribed, then where on earth did Francis get it from? I mean, it's not the sort of thing you can just walk into a chemist and buy!"

"That's true."

We both considered this for a while, then I said, "You don't think—oh no, it's too ridiculous!"

"What?"

"You don't think he might have taken it on purpose ..."

"Committed suicide? Francis? No way! You have to think you're a failure in some way to want to kill yourself. Can you imagine Francis ever considering himself a failure? At anything?"

"Well, no ... but there may have been some reason we don't know about. Some awful thing that might have caused a scandal, or something."

"Seducing choirboys? Embezzling funds? Can you *see* him?"

"Well, when you put it like that, no I can't. Well, if it wasn't an accident and it wasn't suicide, then that leaves ..."

"Murder?"

"It does sound awful when you come out with it just like that."

"You must admit Francis was loathed by a lot of people."

"Well, yes, but that doesn't necessarily make him a candidate for *murder*!"

"More than most, I'd say. Oh well, if it *was* murder then the police will tell us soon enough."

I was just stacking the dishwasher after lunch next day when Mary rang.

"Oh, Sheila," she said, "I thought you'd want to know. Inspector Hosegood's just been. He says they're treating Father's death as a case of murder."

"Oh, Mary!" In spite of my speculations the day before, I was shocked and startled. "What do they think happened?"

"The autopsy showed that the morphine was taken with food, but we haven't got any details yet. I think the inspector is taking things quite slowly and carefully. The cathedral, you know, and the bishop and so on, it's obviously a bit delicate for him."

"Yes, I see. How's your mother taking it?"

"Quite well, considering. Pretty stunned, though."

"And what about Adrian?"

"Oh, Adrian!" There was a definite note of scorn in her voice. "He's still in bed. In shock, the doctor says."

"Oh dear. Well, give Joan my love and tell her if there's anything I can do ..."

"Yes, I will. Thanks, Sheila."

David was in the sitting room brooding over the *Telegraph* crossword puzzle.

"I don't know why I do these things, they only irritate me. 'Size of paper might be topping for a jester'—eight letters?"

"I haven't the faintest idea," I said. "I can't do crosswords, it's like mental arithmetic, my mind goes blank. David, that was Mary. She says that the police are treating it as murder."

David looked up, startled. "Murder!"

"Yes, apparently the morphine was taken with food. I don't know how long it takes to act, whether it was lunch or tea."

"And if it was tea," David said thoughtfully, "then it must have been when I was with him in the cathedral."

"Murder in the cathedral!" I said.

"A singularly difficult play, I always think. Only one decent part and all that tiresome choral speaking, endless special rehearsals. I played Roger Fitzurse once—quite nice to do, but you get a bit fed up just having that scene in the middle and then having to hang about waiting for the curtain call."

David was speaking at random as he usually did when there was something he didn't want to face.

"But *murder*, David!" I exclaimed.

"Yes, well, we did consider the possibility."

"I know, but idle speculation's one thing, the police actually investigating it is another."

I sat down on the arm of the sofa.

"Let's hope it was lunch," I said, "and not tea. But if it

was, what did you have? I mean, *you're* all right, so what did Francis have that you didn't?"

"Oh, heavens, I don't know."

"You must *think*, David, it's important. The police will be asking you."

He made an effort to concentrate. "Right, let me see. Cups of tea, of course, we both had that, and cucumber sandwiches. But there were some other sandwiches—Gentleman's Relish. I remember that because I thought how typically *Francis* it was to have Gentleman's Relish!" He repeated the name with gusto. "I didn't have any of those because I don't like anchovy."

"That might be a possibility," I said. "Anchovy's a strong taste and would hide the taste of anything that was put in it. Go on, was there anything else?"

"Um, let me think ... We both had some of the shortbread and I had a piece of that walnut cake and he had a coffee eclair. Hang on! I've just thought of something! There was that indigestion medicine. He had that before we started tea. Said something about counteracting the acid, something like that. I gather he had it before every meal."

"That's it, then!" I exclaimed. "And, of course, if the tea and the medicine and everything was laid out ready then absolutely *anyone* could have come in and popped something into the medicine—well, anyone who has access to that room, and I daresay quite a lot of the cathedral people did. For all we know, Francis was at loggerheads with half the diocese!"

"That wouldn't surprise me," David said. "Well, dear, it's a comforting theory and one I greatly prefer to the one the police probably have in mind."

"What's that?"

"Who had a tremendous motive for killing Francis? Financial—they always like that—as well as personal. Who was there, on the spot, when he probably imbibed the fatal dose?"

I looked at him in horror.

"Oh no, they couldn't think it was *you*!"

"Well," David said, "I don't expect Inspector Ivor would have thought so, too obvious for him, he was a devious sort of bastard, but I'll lay you even money—or I would if I had any—that I shall be hearing from your nice Inspector Hosegood within the next twenty-four hours."

# 10

Two days elapsed before the inspector rang.

"Good morning, Mrs. Malory. I expect you've heard from Mrs. Beaumont that we are making inquiries into the circumstances of her husband's death. I'd like to have a word with you and Mr. David Beaumont today, if that's convenient."

"Yes, yes, of course. Whenever you like."

"I'll come at about eleven-thirty, then."

"Yes, that will be fine."

David didn't seem too upset at the prospect of the inspector's visit.

"What will you say to him?" I asked. "I mean, how much will you tell him?"

David shrugged. "Well, everything, don't you think, dear? For a start that female, Monica whatsit, will undoubtedly have told him about the quarrel and the raised voices, and I'm sure it will be better to tell him quite openly how it was between Francis and me than for him to worm it out of other people. He'd really think I had something to hide then and he'd be madly suspicious."

"I'm sure you're right," I said. "It's just that—well, anyone who doesn't know you might find the motive very strong ...."

"Let's face it, darling, the motive *was* very strong. I don't say I'd have been prepared to kill Francis—think of all the practical difficulties!—but I can't deny that, in many ways, I'm glad that he's dead."

Inspector Hosegood arrived on the dot of eleven-thirty and accepted my offer of coffee. He and David went into the sitting room and I roamed around the kitchen, fiddling with the coffeemaker, rearranging the cups on the tray and generally working myself up into a nervous state. They seemed to be a very long time and I was reminded of my schooldays, when, on the rare occasions I had committed some misdemeanor (I was a law-abiding child), I had to wait, it seemed interminably, outside the head's study while some other malefactor was interviewed. Eventually David came into the kitchen. He looked rather shaken and simply said, "He'd like to see you now."

I gave him a sympathetic smile and picked up the tray. "There's some coffee there for you, help yourself."

Inspector Hosegood was standing by the window looking up at the hill behind the house.

"Nice view you've got," he said.

"Yes, *aren't* we lucky! It's especially lovely in August and September when the heather and the gorse is out—quite a blaze of color ...." I felt I was babbling as I handed him a cup of coffee and proffered the sugar bowl.

"Yes, I will," he said comfortably. "I know they say it's bad for you nowadays, but I've always had a sweet tooth."

"Do sit down." I gestured to the sofa, but he chose the more upright winged chair, which gave him a magisterial air.

"Well now, Mrs. Malory. Just a few things. Perhaps you could very kindly tell me in your own words about your visit to the deanery the day Mr. Beaumont died."

He sat forward in the chair, nursing his cup, listening intently while I described the events of the afternoon.

"Yes, I see, thank you, that's all very clear. You've known the dean and his family for a long time?"

"Oh yes," I replied. "David, Francis and I were more or less brought up together, though I haven't seen much of Francis in recent years because, quite frankly, I didn't like him. I was fond of Joan, his wife, but Francis was a very difficult person."

"But you've kept in touch with Mr. David Beaumont? He often comes to stay with you?"

"He's always been a close family friend," I said firmly, wondering what exactly the inspector was thinking. "My husband—my late husband—and I have always been very fond of him. He's stayed with us, off and on, for years."

"And this time he came to see his brother?"

"Oh no! Well, he did see Francis, but that wasn't why he came. No, he just needed a little break ..."

"He was in some financial difficulties, I believe?"

I laughed. "All actors have financial difficulties," I said in what I hoped was a light tone, "it goes with the job!"

"But these financial difficulties were worse than usual?"

"Well, yes," I said reluctantly. "But he's always managed to sort things out before and he has many good friends who will help him, I'm sure." I felt I was getting into deep waters and I was relieved to hear a kind of muted bellowing at the window. "Oh, do excuse me! That wretched cat! If I don't let him in he'll drive us mad!"

I went over and opened the window and Foss stalked in. Pausing on the windowsill to stare coldly at the inspector, he jumped down and, with a sideways look to make sure I was watching, began to sharpen his claws on one of the chairs. I picked him up firmly and put him out of the room, apologizing for the interruption.

The inspector laughed. "Little devils, aren't they, Siamese? My sister has one, a real terror, always climbing up the curtains and the stair carpet's in ribbons! My wife says she doesn't know how Josie puts up with it, but my sister always was a fool about animals!"

"I know," I said, "I'm just the same."

"Well now," he went on, "I presume you know that the dean died from morphine poisoning, and we can tell from the autopsy that the substance was taken with the meal he had at about four-thirty, either in the food or, most probably, in the indigestion mixture he took before it. Unfortunately, all the crockery and so forth was taken away and washed up long before we had a chance to get the SOCO people in there. But the fact remains that he does seem to have taken the morphine during the course of that meal he had with his brother."

"Yes," I said cautiously.

"There were two occasions when the dean was out of the room. He went down into the main body of the cathedral to see, first, the precentor and then the archdeacon. The first time he left the room they hadn't started tea and the dean hadn't taken the medicine."

"You mean there was just one opportunity for David to put morphine in the medicine! Honestly, Inspector, it's just not possible! David simply isn't that sort of person—well, you've met him!"

"But wouldn't you say," the inspector said, looking at me quizzically, "that being an actor means pretending to be someone you're not?"

"But not David!" I exclaimed. "He's almost transparently honest—that's always been his trouble. Anyway, I've known him forever—long before he became an actor—and he's always been the same."

"I'm sure you're right, Mrs. Malory. I was just thinking aloud, you might say."

"Anyway," I continued, "the tea was laid out already. Anyone could have gone in and tampered with it."

"Hardly anyone."

"Well, anyone who knew it was there."

"I'm afraid that's not actually so," Inspector Hosegood

said. "A Mrs. Woodward, who was on duty in that part of the building that afternoon, said that she didn't see anyone go into that room before the dean, Mr. Beaumont and yourself arrived. She also told me that while Mr. Beaumont was with his brother there were sounds of a violent quarrel."

"Oh, Monica Woodward!" I exclaimed. "She's a terrible gossip with a highly developed sense of the dramatic. Violent quarrel! I believe David was very annoyed with Francis—he will have told you about that, I'm sure—and he may have raised his voice a little, but *violent*, no!"

"She also said that Mr. David Beaumont left in anger."

"I daresay he did," I said. "I'm not at all surprised. Francis could be really impossible sometimes and the provocation was very great, and David's put up with it for years and never said anything. In fact, this is the first time I've ever known him to lose his temper with Francis!"

I stopped, suddenly aware that I had somehow been trapped into a remark that was less than helpful to David's case.

"So he did lose his temper?" the inspector said.

"If you call it losing his temper to tell Francis a few home truths that he should have done years ago," I said spiritedly, "yes he did. But it was quite out of character."

"People do behave out of character, I believe, when they're under stress."

"But there is one thing," I said quickly. "If David had been going to do a devious thing like poisoning his brother, then he would hardly have had a 'violent quarrel' with him on the very afternoon he was proposing to kill him, now would he?"

Inspector Hosegood smiled at me benevolently. "That thought had occurred to me, too, Mrs. Malory. Though, I suppose if he was *really* clever it might be a good double bluff!"

I laughed reluctantly. "I can see that you've got an answer for everything, Inspector."

"Not everything, not by a long chalk. Not yet, anyway." He stood up and put his coffee cup down on a table. "I believe you are a friend of Inspector Eliot, here at Taviscombe?"

"Why yes," I said in some surprise. "He's married to my goddaughter."

"He tells me," the inspector continued, "that you have a very good eye for details and a very good idea about what makes people tick."

"Did he!" I exclaimed. "Goodness!"

"He said that you'd given him quite a lot of help on some of his cases, one way or another."

"Well, I did a bit, I suppose."

"I just thought," he said, "that if you do happen to notice anything, or if something occurs to you, then I'd be glad to hear from you ... let me give you my number."

I took the piece of paper and said, "Of course. I'll be only too pleased to do whatever I can to clear up this dreadful thing."

"Inspector Eliot said you had a highly developed sense of curiosity." Inspector Hosegood looked at me sideways to see how I was taking this remark.

"Oh dear," I laughed, "that sounds rather awful!"

"I think he found it quite useful." He moved toward the door. "Good-bye, Mrs. Malory. Thank you for the coffee."

I found David in the kitchen, perched uncomfortably on a stool, brooding over an empty coffee cup.

"Well," I asked, "how did you get on?"

"I honestly don't know. The inspector doesn't give much away."

"I know. Here, let me give you another cup of coffee."

"He said that Francis was poisoned by something he had at teatime, when we were alone together."

"Yes, that's what he told me."

"And it's perfectly true that Francis did go out of the

room twice, so I suppose in theory I *could* have popped something into the sandwiches or the coffee eclairs." He shook a couple of sweeteners into his coffee and stirred it vigorously. "Which definitely makes me number one suspect."

"I don't see why," I said. "After all, you didn't *make* the sandwiches. Joan did. And they may well have sat around in the kitchen at the deanery where any member of that family could have got at them. The same applies to the indigestion mixture, which, incidentally, is where the inspector seems to think the morphine was put."

"Well, yes," David said, "but Joan and the others haven't got the sort of motive I have for wanting to kill Francis, have they?"

"I wouldn't say that!" I said firmly. "Think of all the misery and repression in that household—it's like something out of *The Barretts of Wimpole Street*! Years and years of accumulated frustration and unhappiness. It's a wonder they didn't murder him ages ago!"

David laughed reluctantly. "It wasn't the happiest of families, I know, but I'm sure the inspector will latch onto the money thing, the police always do."

"Well, we don't know what financial motive there may have been as well," I said. "I mean, how did Francis leave his money? There must have been a lot of it. I know Mary wanted to set up in partnership with her chum in those stables. She'd need quite a bit for that. And we have no idea what Adrian's financial situation is. There are lots of other possibilities. Come on, cheer up! Inspector Hosegood seems to me like a sensible man, not the sort who would jump to obvious conclusions."

"Well, I hope not. Do you know, he remembered Inspector Ivor! He asked me in a jokey way how I thought he would have tackled this case!"

"What did you say?"

"I said that Ivor was never one to go for the obvious and that the murderer would probably turn out to be one of the minor canons, a sinister figure from Francis's past!"

"Well," I said, going over to put the empty cups into the dishwasher, "you never know. All sorts of people have pasts stuffed full of sinister figures. It seems to me like a wide open case, endless possibilities. After all, with a person as disagreeable as Francis there may well be masses of people who wanted to kill him. It's just a question of finding ways they could have got at that food and I'm sure we can do that if we set our minds to it."

"What do you mean?" David asked suspiciously. "If we set our minds to it?"

"There's no reason why we shouldn't poke about a bit ourselves, ask a few questions. After all," I said virtuously, "the inspector did ask me to keep my eyes open."

# 11

I'd gone into Woolworth's to get some more lightbulbs (isn't it extraordinary how they always seem to go in *pairs*?) and I was wandering aimlessly around the aisles as I always do in this particular store, a hangover, I suppose, from the days of my childhood, when nearly every Saturday morning I'd prowl around the counters trying to decide what to spend my pocket money on.

By the piled-up beach balls and other toys I saw two familiar figures. "Hello, Roger," I said, "are you spending your day off child-minding?"

Roger Eliot—Inspector Roger Eliot of the Taviscombe CID and husband of my goddaughter Jilly—turned and said with a rueful smile, "As you see! Jilly's taken Alex to the clinic so I said I'd look after Delia. I always forget what hard work small children are! In fact, I have to admit, we're here to purchase a bribe."

"It's often the only way," I agreed. "Hello, Delia, what are you going to choose?"

"I have this dolly," Delia said decisively, clutching a box containing a flaxen-haired doll with wholesome, retroussé features and dressed in a flowered dirndl dress.

"That's a pretty one," I said, looking at it. "Made in China. How extraordinary, they've all got blond plaits and blue eyes. I wonder if the Chinese think all Western children look like something out of *The Sound of Music*!"

"Are you sure you want another doll?" Roger asked. He turned to me and said, "She's got about twenty dolls already, the house is full of them! Jilly will go mad if we go back with another one."

Delia shook her head. "Want *this* dolly," she said firmly.

"How about this nice book?" Roger suggested. "Or these lovely crayons?"

"Want this dolly," Delia repeated, this time with a hint of tears in her voice.

"All right," Roger said hastily, "we'll get the dolly."

We all three made our way to the cash desk, Delia, now restored to smiles, telling me about her other dolls.

"The naughty dollies pulled the heads off all the *flowers*," she said confidentially, "and they spilled Mummy's perfume all over the floor—it was *everywhere*. They were very *naughty* dollies and I had to smack them. Not Patty-doll," she amended, "*she* didn't spill perfume, only Raggy-doll and Betsy-doll and Mary-doll and Jane-doll ..." The litany continued until we were outside the shop.

"What are you going to do now?" I asked.

"We've got some bread to feed the seagulls," Roger said. "Do you feel like coming too?"

"All right," I said. "I haven't fed the seagulls for years, not, come to think of it, since Michael was little."

"You'd better get in training for when you're a grandmother."

"No sign of that yet," I said regretfully. "I often wonder if Michael will ever settle down."

We made our way through the town to the seafront and picked our way carefully down the seaweedy steps onto the beach. The tide was out and the sand was dry and crunchy under our feet. Roger gave Delia some pieces of bread and tried to show her how to throw them toward the seagulls, who, seeing a bag opened, had gathered hopefully in some numbers. But Delia's small, inexpert hands couldn't throw the bread far enough, though one gull, braver than its fellows, swooped in and took a crust almost from under her feet, causing her to cry out in alarm and hide behind her father.

So Roger and I enjoyed ourselves, tossing bread in the air as high as we could so the gulls came circling and diving, calling shrilly, while Delia ran about laughing and shouting with excitement.

"There," Roger said, when all the bread was gone and the birds had departed in search of other patrons, "wasn't that fun!"

"Simple pleasures are the best," I agreed, laughing. "And, actually, I could do with a bit of pleasure at the moment. You know about Francis Beaumont? Of course you do—Inspector Hosegood said you'd discussed it."

"Yes, we were both at a divisional meeting and he told me about the case then."

"He came to see David and me yesterday," I said. "It seems that David was actually there when it happened. And, of course, he *did* have a motive for killing his brother, I can understand why the inspector's suspicious. But David wasn't the only one, by any means ...."

"I thought you might have a few thoughts on the subject," Roger said, looking at me quizzically. "That's why I suggested that Hosegood should have a talk with you—apart from the fact that you were at the deanery anyway."

"He said you'd had a word."

"Hosegood's a shrewd man," Roger said, "don't let that bucolic appearance fool you. He agrees with me that knowing the people concerned and the general setup is very important—things the police can't be expected to know about. I told him how useful your particular sort of curiosity has been to me in the past and he was very interested."

"If I can help in any way, of course I will. And I do have one advantage over the police."

"What's that?"

"*I* know that David didn't do it—so that's one person eliminated."

Roger smiled. "You should never get carried away by your personal feelings in any investigation."

"You can't have it both ways," I said. "It's the way I feel about people, from my own knowledge of them, that makes me able to investigate them, as you put it. If you've known someone for ages you're far more likely to know what sort of person he or she really is and what sort of thing they'd be capable of."

"Well, do what you can."

Delia, who had been splashing about in the rock pools, rushed over to her father and clasped him lovingly around the knees.

"Oh, heavens, look at her dress, it's absolutely *soaked*. We'd better go back and get her changed before Jilly sees it!"

"Ice cream," Delia chanted, "ice cream, ice cream."

"Yes, all right," Roger said placatingly, "we'll get an ice cream on the way back." He looked at me defensively. "Yes, I know," he said, "I'm spoiling her!"

I laughed. "I think it's sweet. My father always used to spoil me—that's what fathers are for."

Roger hoisted his daughter onto his shoulders and we went up onto the promenade where an ice-cream van was always strategically parked.

"Right," I said, "I'll leave you to it."

"Good hunting," Roger said. "Hosegood really will listen to anything you find out, or even any theories you may have. He's sensible enough to accept help from any quarter."

I told David what Roger had said while we were having lunch.

"I don't know," David said doubtfully. "I mean, poking about in other people's lives!"

"Look," I said, putting an extra spoonful of kedgeree

onto his plate, "I'm fond of Joan and Mary, and even Adrian, though I've never known him very well, but I'm fonder of you! And as long as the police think you killed Francis we've simply got to find reasons why other people had equally good motives. What's wrong with that?"

"When you put it like that ... But how on earth does one go about it?"

"You ask me that! After all those years of being Inspector Ivor!"

"I had a script, dear, I didn't make it up as I went along!"

"Right," I said briskly, "then, if necessary, we'll provide you with a script."

"Anyhow, Inspector Ivor had all the police paraphernalia behind him. We're just civilians."

"Actually, that's our strength. What we do is simply go over to Culminster and talk to people, just casually. You'd be surprised what you can find out from a little idle chat!"

"Well," David said doubtfully, "I'll do my best, but you'll have to tell me what to do and what to ask."

"You don't actually *ask*," I explained, "you sort of let things emerge. Would you like a banana or a piece of cake or just coffee?"

"Coffee, please. Then after this I must go out and order some flowers for Nana."

"Are you all right for money?" I asked tentatively.

"Yes, bless you, dear. Julian sent me the check for this month's rent today so I'm fine. I must say, I'll be glad after tomorrow when the funeral's over and done with."

Because Francis had made all the arrangements for Nana's funeral and had intended to take part in the service himself, the whole thing had been postponed because of his death, which had somehow added to our feelings of uncertainty and disorientation.

"I did tell you, didn't I, that Joan rang to say that, if we didn't mind, she wouldn't be coming."

"Yes. It would have been a bit stressful for the poor soul. So I expect it'll be just us."

It wasn't quite. There were several old ladies who sat together in a pew at the back and an old man with a hearing aid who came into the front pew with David and me. Although it was quite a bright day and shafts of brilliant sunlight made patterns on the floor of the nave, the church felt cold. The words of the service seemed to fall heavily on our ears in that empty space and, during the Twenty-third Psalm, while we were saying "Yea, though I walk through the valley of the shadow of death," a cloud moved across the sun and the light in the church was momentarily quenched. I shivered and I felt David stiffen beside me.

After the service, I half expected the old man to get into the funeral car with us to go to the cemetery, but he shuffled off with one of the elderly ladies and we never did find out who he was ("Perhaps he's hired by the undertakers," David said, "the modern equivalent of the funeral mute!"). So it was just David and me at the graveside as the clergyman spoke the solemn words of the committal.

Taviscombe Cemetery is a pleasant place, surrounded by hills, which the early ling was just touching with purple; sheep were grazing and, with the sound of the traffic on the road outside muted by a line of fine poplars, it was very peaceful. When the vicar had gone, we stood for a moment, looking at the wreaths: one from David, one from Michael and me, one from Joan, Mary and Adrian, and a sheaf of flowers with a card that read "Happy Memories, Esme, from Edith and Lily." I was glad that there was some recognition that Nana had been a person in her own right, with a life and friends of her own.

David sighed. "Poor Nana. I keep remembering how devoted she was to my father. All the difficulties came from that—it was only her love for him. I should have been more patient."

"You were always very good to her," I said, taking his arm consolingly, "and she was fond of you, you know she was. And she did get very peculiar toward the end."

"Well, perhaps she *is* better 'out of the miseries of the sinful world,' " David said. Then, as we moved away toward the car, he went on more cheerfully, "You know, I've played so many clergymen in my time, I felt, in a way, *I* should have been taking the service and I found myself saying the words under my breath! Is that sacrilegious, I wonder?"

"How did it go?" Michael asked that evening. "Sorry I couldn't come, but there was this client I had to see in Taunton."

"Sad, of course," I replied, "as these things always are, especially when there are so few people there."

"I don't expect she had much of a social life," David said, "and almost all the people she knew when she was young have died. It must be awful to outlive your own generation."

"I'm afraid it'll be a little time before you can expect to sort out the house," Michael said, "what with the inquest and the police investigation, not to mention the whole business of probate. I should imagine Mortimer and Shaw were Francis's solicitors—they're the largest firm in Culminster and do a lot of cathedral business."

"Surely the bank will hold their collective hand," I said, "now that you can tell them that the house really is going onto the market and can be a proper security for your loan." A sudden thought struck me. "Anyway, don't you own the whole thing now that Francis is dead?"

"Yes, I suppose I do, that's what Father's will said—if the house hadn't already been sold, then the survivor would inherit the whole thing."

"Well, that's fine, then. I'm sure the bank will be reasonable."

"Oh dear, though," David said ruefully, "it does rather increase my motive. I don't think the inspector will like that at all!"

"All the more reason," I said, "for making our own investigations."

"Now do be careful, Ma!" Michael said warningly. He turned to David, "She's terrible when she gets the bit between her teeth and goes plunging about pretending to be a private eye."

"I'm only going to chat to a few people in Culminster," I said defensively. "Joan and Mary and Adrian. Oh yes, and if I go over there tomorrow, I should be able to have a word with Monica Woodward. I think it's her day for being on duty in the cathedral."

"What on earth do you expect to get out of *her*?" David asked. "I thought she was a witness for the prosecution."

"Oh, I don't know," I said vaguely, "something useful might emerge."

"Actually," David said, "I really must get my hair cut tomorrow, so if you don't mind ..."

I've noticed, over the years, that men always seem to need to have their hair cut when some activity is proposed in which they don't wish to participate.

"Coward!" I said. "Still, I may well do better without you."

# 12

I was lucky to find a parking space quite near to the cathedral. I didn't particularly want to go into the close and park at the deanery, since I wasn't really sure I'd want to go and see Joan. It was too soon after lunch for there to be many visitors and the great building was very quiet. As I made my way down the nave, I glanced up at the triforium, the upper story above the aisle, with its bays of stone vaulting, and thought how strange it was that something as ugly as murder should have taken place behind that beautiful facade.

I was glad to see that Monica was on duty, sitting at her table reading what appeared to be some sort of diocesan newsletter. She looked up and exclaimed in surprise, "Sheila! Fancy seeing you! Have you come to look at the library?"

"Well no, not as such," I said, having prepared my excuse in advance. "I've really come to see Mary. I imagine she's still working in the muniment room, isn't she?"

"Yes, she's still there. Though I had heard"—Monica leaned forward to impart what she felt was confidential information—"that she's thinking of leaving. Too many sad memories, I suppose. Quite understandable. But, of course, the whole family will have to find somewhere else to live. Dreadful for them, to have to be thinking of such a thing at a time like this!"

"Yes, poor Joan, she must feel it terribly."

"I couldn't believe it, when they told me," Monica went

on, her prominent blue eyes positively bulging with excitement. "The dean dead! The police everywhere, questioning people. And then when they said it was murder! Well!"

"I don't think they've actually decided that it was murder," I said. "It might be accidental death."

"Morphine, that's what I heard. You don't go taking something like that accidentally, now do you?"

"Well ..."

"No, it's obvious someone killed him, poor man. From all the questions the police asked *me*"—she emphasized the word to indicate her own importance in the investigation—"it looks as if they thought it happened right *here*, that afternoon you and his brother came."

"It is possible."

She looked around melodramatically to make sure that we were alone and said, "A terrible quarrel, it was, shouting! You wouldn't believe! Well, the brother was, I couldn't hear what the dean was saying, all about money. And, of course"—Monica leaned back, her lips set in an emphatic grimace—"when families fall out about money ..."

"So you heard it all?" I asked.

She looked a little disconcerted. "I couldn't help hearing," she said. "As I said, there were raised voices, shouting. And then he—the brother, that is—rushed out, slammed the door right in the dean's face. Very nasty! Here in the cathedral! I was quite upset."

"I'm sure you must have been," I said soothingly. "So you were able to tell the police exactly what happened?"

"Oh yes, they said I'd been really helpful."

"I'm sure."

"You see, I was on duty here all afternoon, all the time. Right from when Mrs. Beaumont brought all the tea things over, until the dean went away after his brother left."

"Oh, did Mrs. Beaumont bring the food over herself?"

"Oh yes, she always did. Such a nice woman. Just between ourselves," Monica confided, "I wouldn't say she was what I'd call a very good manager—I know the dean felt that sometimes—but she was devoted to *him*."

"And after that," I said casually, "no one else went into the dean's room until we arrived?"

"That's right," she said emphatically, "no one else."

"Well," I said, "it was lucky for the police that you were on duty that day and that you were so observant."

"Oh, you have to keep your eyes open when you're on duty here." She laughed. "You wouldn't *believe* some of the things people do!"

"I can imagine." I felt that I had probed enough and leaned forward to admire the small bowl of flowers on the table. "What a lovely arrangement! One of yours, I'm sure."

"How kind of you to say so! Yes, it is one of mine. I do rather pride myself—I go to classes, actually, and one of the instructors there did say that my work was really quite up to professional standards."

"This is absolutely beautiful, and I know that you do some of the cathedral flowers?"

A shadow crossed her face. "I am on the rota," she said, "but they've only given me that place by the west door. Mrs. Harrington-Jones—she's in charge of the rota—*never* lets me do the screen or either of the transepts and, of course, she and that friend of hers Mrs. Bingham always do the altar flowers. I said to Betty Fisher only the other day that it really wasn't fair, I'm sure our work is just as good as theirs—better, if you ask me! Betty did a really beautiful arrangement for the Lady Chapel last week—yellow lilies, those Esther Reed daisies and eucalyptus, it was really quite striking! And, do you know, Mrs. Harrington-Jones had the cheek to tell her that it wasn't 'important' enough for that position. Would you believe it!"

"No! What an extraordinary thing!"

Monica seemed gratified by my response and went on,

"Poor Betty was ever so surprised and very upset—well, you can imagine—and she asked me to go down and have a look myself, since I do have a lot of experience, and I told her it was quite exquisite—very like one of those arrangements in that Constance Spry book. How that Mrs. Harrington-Jones had the nerve! Anyway"—she flashed me a look of triumph—"the dean himself said how nice it was. He was just passing the Lady Chapel on his way up here before you and his brother came ..."

She broke off in some confusion and we sat looking at each other for a moment in silence as the implication of what she had just said dawned on us both, then I said quickly, "Still, I expect you were only away for a little while?"

"Oh yes," she agreed eagerly, "and I'm sure I'd have seen if anyone went up that staircase ..."

"I'm sure you would," I said. "So the dean thought the flower arrangement was all right?"

She returned to the subject of the flowers gratefully.

"He said he thought they would grace any part of the cathedral. Wasn't that nice! Oh, he was a lovely man, so distinguished looking, he'll be greatly missed."

"Yes," I said, "things will be quite different without him."

I longed to get away to consider this new turn of events, but felt I must make at least a show of looking for Mary.

"Well," I said, "I'd better get on." I opened my handbag. "Perhaps I'd better have a ticket for the library."

"Oh, if you're just going through to have a word with Mary I don't think we need make you buy a ticket!" She gave me a conspiratorial smile which I did my best to return.

"Oh, really? Thanks so much! I'll just pop through, then."

I went through the great oak door and came upon Mary straight away, sitting at a table just inside the library, flicking in a desultory way through a card index.

"Hello, Mary," I said, "how splendid to see one of those

old-fashioned things! I suppose it won't be long before all that's on a computer, even here!"

"Sheila!" Mary looked up in surprise. "How nice to see you. Yes, I suppose so. Father had a computer in his room up here, of course, but it would look rather out of place in these surroundings!" She gestured to the high stone vaulting of the ceiling and the intricately carved window embrasures, the heavy oak doors and bookcases, and, in pride of place, the great, leather-bound chained Bible on its ornate brass stand.

Mary got up and pushed forward a chair. "Do sit down. Have you been to see Mother? I'm afraid she's out today. She's gone to see Miss Burgess—her brother old Canon Burgess died a couple of weeks ago."

"Oh dear, I am sorry," I said. "I had no idea—I must have missed the announcement in the *Telegraph*. He was such a sweet man!"

"He was my godfather," Mary said, "and we were all very fond of him. He'd been ill for quite a while—he was in dreadful pain at the end—but Miss Burgess insisted on keeping him at home, because she knew how he hated the idea of going into hospital."

"Poor Evelyn!" I said. "It must have been very exhausting for her."

"We've always thought she was very vague and rather scatty, but she does seem to have managed very well. Mother was over there a lot and did all she could to help and, of course, Father was there at the end. But now, poor soul, she's feeling very lonely—there were just the two of them, no other relatives—so Mother feels she must spend some time with her. I think it helps her to feel needed. She'll be sorry to have missed you."

"It wasn't anything special," I said, "just that I had to come over to Culminster on an errand for Michael so I thought I'd pop in and see how you all were. How is your mother?"

Mary shrugged. "A bit like Miss Burgess, I suppose, missing Father."

"Yes, of course. And in such dreadful circumstances."

"The police have been quite good, really. Once they'd taken our statements they left us alone. But it's early days yet."

"You've no idea," I asked tentatively, "if they've made any progress?"

"Well, they haven't said anything to me. We'll have to wait for the inquest." She spoke the word without any emotion. "Perhaps we'll hear something then."

"Yes, perhaps you will."

We sat in silence for a moment, Mary fiddling with the card index.

"How's Adrian?" I asked.

"A bit better—that's why Mother was able to go over and see Miss Burgess. He's gone back to the office."

"It really did seem to hit him very hard."

Mary gave a little snort of contempt. "He simply went to pieces, quite useless. I just hope he'll buck up his ideas soon and get down to sorting out Father's papers. I shall need to know how things stand financially so I can get on with my partnership in the stables."

"You're definitely leaving here, then?" I asked. "Don't you enjoy the work at all?"

"I can't wait to leave! Oh, it's not the work—actually I quite like it here, especially now I don't have Father breathing down my neck! Do you know, that very day, the day he ... he died, he insisted on going over the figures I'd worked out for the restoration work we need on some of the old books here—I mean, I'd got it perfectly well sorted out, but he couldn't even trust me to do a simple thing like that without checking up on me!"

"Oh dear! I do see what you mean."

"Anyway, I've always wanted to work full-time with Fay at the stables. It's something I've *longed* for!"

"And something you'll do very well," I said, "you're so good with nervous riders. Look how well you coped with me!"

"I hope you'll come again soon," Mary said.

"Now I've got over the stiffness," I laughed.

"Well, if you were to ride regularly you wouldn't be stiff."

"I know. Perhaps when David's gone back to Stratford. I love having him here and he couldn't be an easier guest, but even one's dearest friends do take up *time*! Still, I suppose the police won't want him to leave Taviscombe until they've got some sort of result."

"You mean they suspect *Uncle David*!" Mary looked at me in astonishment.

"Of course, it's ridiculous, really, to anyone who knows him, but from their point of view he does have the strongest motive—money! And he did have that quarrel with your father that afternoon *and* he was there when your father ate or drank whatever it was that had the morphine in it."

"Ye-es, I can see how it all looks suspicious. But, for instance, where do they think Uncle David got the morphine *from*?"

"Goodness alone knows!" I replied. "I suppose they'd just say oh, he's an actor, isn't he, and don't they all take drugs!"

"I shouldn't think Inspector Hosegood would be so naive," Mary said. "He struck me as being very much on the ball."

"Yes, I thought so too. Still, with a perfectly good motive like David's I suppose they don't feel the need to look elsewhere. I mean, who else would want to kill your father? I don't suppose there's a disgruntled verger or a canon with a grievance?"

"Well, he didn't exactly arouse friendly feelings in the other clergy," Mary said, "but then, as far as I know he didn't excite strong enough passions to justify murder either."

Since the only other suspects were members of Mary's own family—indeed, Mary herself—I didn't feel I could continue this particular speculation.

"Well," I said, gathering up my handbag and preparing to leave, "tell your mother I'm sorry to have missed her. I suppose sometime you'll all have to think about moving. If there's anything I can do to help, with the packing up and so forth, please do say. I know what a tedious business it can be. Are she and Adrian really going to move into that cottage near the stables?"

"Oh yes," Mary said, "it's much the best solution."

"You don't think that Adrian might want to have a place of his own?"

"You mean now that Father's dead and can't make him live at home anymore?"

"Oh dear, is that how it was?"

"Very much so. Adrian's lived in Father's shadow for so long that I think he's lost the will to make any sort of life for himself. He's just a cipher."

"Well, you're not," I said, "you've kept your independent spirit."

"I tried to stand up to him. Not often"—Mary gave a short laugh—"and not very successfully, but I suppose I've got a bit of Father in me. Adrian takes after Mother."

"Yes, I think you're right. You'll be able to look after them both if they're near at hand."

She laughed again. "Someone will have to."

"Well, don't let your sense of responsibility be a burden—you've your own life to lead."

"Oh, I'll lead my own life, don't you worry! I can't *tell* you the sense of freedom, the feeling of exhilaration! I've never felt really alive until now!" She looked at me quizzically. "Have I shocked you? Actually saying things like that when my father's just been killed! But it would be hypocritical to pretend that I'm sad when I'm so very definitely not. You do see that, Sheila, don't you? You know how he stultified our lives, you know we're all better off now he's gone."

"Yes," I said thoughtfully as I moved toward the door. "I can see how you might be."

I smiled good-bye to Monica (briskly telling two foreign students that they couldn't take their backpacks into the library) and made my way carefully down the stone steps. As I passed the Lady Chapel I glanced inside. The arrangement of yellow lilies had gone and instead there was an enormous, florid confection of gladioli, iris and chrysanthemums. Apparently Mrs. Harrington-Jones had triumphed after all.

# 13

"So you see," I concluded triumphantly, "*anyone* could have gone into Francis's room and poisoned the medicine!"

"Well, hardly anyone," David protested mildly.

"Well, you know what I mean. It certainly opens the field up quite a bit—it doesn't have to be you or the rest of the family."

"But who, and why?"

"I don't know, but there may have been any number of reasons. He may have been having an affair with someone."

"Francis! That sanctimonious pillar of the establishment? Murdered by a jealous husband? Never!" David laughed.

"You don't know," I said, "the most unlikely people ..."

"It's a lovely thought, dear, and it gives me great pleasure to contemplate, but I fear not."

"Well then," I said, "how about if Francis knew something about someone, something that would ruin their lives, and he was going to speak out about it."

"I must admit that's much more likely," David replied. "I can just imagine him talking about his duty and the truth needing to be told and guff like that. *Very* Francis!"

"There you are, then. I think I'd better try and get the inspector on the phone right away."

"The inspector?"

"Yes, to tell him that Monica wasn't doing her Cerberus-guarding-the-gates-of-hell act all afternoon as she said."

"But ..."

"I have to, Monica would never tell him herself, she'd be too embarrassed and wouldn't like to lose face."

"I suppose so," David said reluctantly, "but it seems a bit—well, you know!"

"A bit like sneaking—what those nice young people in Australian soaps call 'dobbing in'? I suppose it might, but if, by telling the inspector, I can take his mind off you—and Joan and Mary and Adrian too, don't forget—then I must certainly do it."

"Well, if you put it like that ..."

I got through to Inspector Hosegood straight away and told him about Monica's absence.

"I thought I'd better let you know," I said, adding mendaciously, "I don't know if Mrs. Woodward realized how important it was."

I sensed Inspector Hosegood's appreciation of this amendment.

"Yes, well, thank you, Mrs. Malory. It does put a slightly different complexion on things. Now then, the Lady Chapel, you say? Just a minute, I've got a plan of the cathedral here ... Yes, I see. Quite a way from the stairs to the library and the dean's room."

"And if they were looking at the flowers," I said, "they'd be right inside the chapel and they certainly couldn't see anyone from there."

"Yes, I see. Right, then, Mrs. Malory, thank you for your help."

"I don't suppose you've any news?" I asked, unwilling to be dismissed quite so quickly.

"We are following up a few things. Actually, I had been meaning to get in touch—I'd be grateful if Mr. David Beaumont would come along to the station. There are a couple of things that I'd like to go over with him. Do you think he could manage tomorrow?"

"Yes," I said, rather disconcerted by this further interest in David. "I don't think he's doing anything in particular. What time?"

"Eleven-thirty, if that's convenient."

"Yes, right, I'll drive him over."

"Thank you, Mrs. Malory, that would be fine."

"It's a bit much," I said to David, when I'd passed on the inspector's message. "I open up a whole new vista of suspects for him and all he can do is ask to see you again!"

"I wonder what he wants?" David said uneasily. "He went through things pretty thoroughly when he came here and then again when we both went to the police station to sign our statements."

"Oh well, you'll know tomorrow. While you're with him I'll go and see Joan and you can come around to the deanery when you've finished."

"If I'm not languishing in jail by then," David said gloomily. "I don't like the sound of this at all."

"Oh, it's probably something perfectly simple, something new he's discovered, perhaps, that he wants to check against your statement."

"Yes," David replied gloomily, "but *what*?"

"Well done, Ma," Michael said at supper, "that was a neat bit of sleuthing. It opens up all sorts of possibilities. Personally, I'm all for the theory that horrible Francis was having a torrid affair."

"David thinks he was too puritanical."

"Oh, they're often the worst! You should see the evidence we get in some divorce cases! Anyway, it's fairly classic—look at that chap in Shakespeare."

"Which chap?"

"That one in the play with the girl and her brother—you know."

"I think he means *Measure for Measure*," David said, making a giant intuitive leap. "Yes, you might cast Francis as Angelo—a marvelous part but hellishly difficult, especially that ending—practically no one's really got away with it. Perhaps John G."

"I still think money, really," I said. "Francis must have been pretty well off, in spite of all that guff he gave to you, David, about cash flows and so on. I saw a great list of shares and things on the computer printout on his desk. Perhaps he did someone down over a business deal? I mean, everyone said how clever he was with money, and people who are clever with money are often devious—look at all those fraud cases in the City!" I got up and started to clear away the pudding plates. "Shall we have coffee outside? It's a lovely evening."

"Anyway," I said, when we were sitting on the veranda, "I know Mary desperately wanted money for those stables, and I wouldn't be surprised if Adrian needed cash as well. I haven't heard anything about the will. How long will it take to be proved, Michael?"

"Depends who does it. Actually, a deucedly rum thing happened about Francis's will."

Michael and his fellow assistant solicitor, Philip, have taken to playing at being Dickensian lawyers. This involves the use of archaic language, exaggerated Old World courtesies and the wearing of double-breasted waistcoats—a harmless eccentricity, though one that can become a little tiresome for the innocent bystander.

"What sort of thing?"

"Well, Dick Wisbech came over to see us about something today. He's with Mortimer and Shaw, and I was right, they were Francis's solicitors. Anyway, Dick and I went to have a pie and a pint at lunchtime and we were chatting and, of course, the murder at the deanery cropped up—as you can imagine, the whole of Culminster's agog!"

"So?"

"So it's all most peculiar. A couple of months ago Francis wrote to Bernard Mortimer and said that he was withdrawing his affairs."

"Goodness!" I exclaimed. "Did he say why?"

"No explanation at all."

"So who are his solicitors now?" David asked. "I suppose I ought to get in touch with them about—well, about *things*."

"No one knows," Michael said. "Francis simply asked for all the documents relating to his affairs to be sent to him at the deanery. Since then, not a whisper of him going to anyone else, which is very odd indeed, because usually these things get about—especially when there are unusual circumstances."

"How extraordinary!" I waved ineffectually at a couple of midges that were hovering around my head. "So what do you think?"

"I don't know what to think and Dick Wisbech can't imagine, either. Vastly intriguing!"

"Perhaps it's something to do with Adrian," I suggested. "You know, him being an accountant."

"Accountants, my dear Mama," Michael said condescendingly, "are *quite* different from solicitors. Since both your husband and your son were solicitors I do feel you should have known that."

"Idiot! No, what I meant was that perhaps Francis was engaged in some sort of business that he didn't want his solicitors to know about. I mean, they might be acting for him in financial matters, agreements or something—I'm not sure how these things are worked out. Tax, perhaps—I know your father used to have to deal with some tax things for his clients—anyway, perhaps there was something not quite, well, ethical. Francis might have wanted Adrian to wangle things for him somehow."

Michael put his fingertips together in a formal, judicial manner. "It's possible. Though Adrian's pretty wet. I wouldn't think he'd be bright enough for any sort of fiddle."

"But Francis was," David said, "and he could have guided the wretched Adrian along the paths of unrighteousness."

"I wonder?" Michael looked thoughtful. "But even so, I don't see how all this has anything to do with Francis's *murder*."

"It might, somehow, give Adrian a motive," I said. "He might have rebelled against what his father was doing. No, that's no good. The trouble is I don't really know much about Adrian. He's such a nonperson, if you know what I mean. Do we know anyone who knows him?"

"Actually, Philip was at school with him," Michael said. "I'll see what he makes of him."

"Meanwhile," I urged, "see if you can find out anything else on the legal and financial front. I don't see at the moment how it all fits in, but something as odd as this business with his solicitor must have *some* bearing on Francis's murder."

I had a bad night. For no apparent reason. Usually I sleep like a log, zonking straight out, my book often slipping from my hand and the light still on. Every so often, though, I just can't get off. I toss and turn, try to remember all the relaxation exercises I did in my antenatal classes before Michael was born, turn the light on and read for a bit, even, occasionally, count imaginary sheep. But in the end I always have to reconcile myself to lying there, letting my thoughts roam at will, wide awake.

Not surprisingly, I suppose, I thought about Francis and who might have murdered him. For all that I had gone on about anyone being in a position to kill Francis now we knew Monica hadn't been on guard, I still felt, in my heart, that the murderer was most likely to have been one of the family. I knew it wasn't David so that left Joan, Mary and Adrian. Mary had a very strong motive. She was desperate to break away from her father's powerful influence and she needed money to put into the stables. Actually, I was pretty sure it wasn't simply a business arrangement that she wished for with Fay. And that, of course, was another reason for wanting her father dead. There was no way he would have countenanced that sort of relationship, there would have been dreadful scenes, and Joan as well as Mary would have been the subject of Francis's wrath. I shuddered even to think of it!

There was no doubt, too, that Mary actively hated her father. As far as I could see, there had never been any expression of love in that family and Mary, a sensitive and basically affectionate girl, had been starved of any sort of loving relationship, since I knew that Francis, as well as never showing affection himself, had always frowned on any overt display of emotion between Joan and the children. I remember once we had all been on a picnic (I can't remember the unlikely circumstances that brought us together for such an event) when Michael, Mary and Adrian were all small. The children had gone off on their own (led by Michael since the other two would never have thought of such an independent action) and were playing by a stream in a nearby field. Suddenly we heard Mary shrieking and they all three rushed up to us. Mary and Adrian clung to Joan and Michael nearly knocked Peter over as he clutched him in terror. "There was a bull!" Michael cried. "He chased us!"

Mary was still sobbing and Adrian, huddled close to his mother, was white with fear. Peter and I reassured Michael as best we could and comforted him, but Francis snapped at Joan, who had Mary in her arms, "Put the child down at once, Joan! Mary, Adrian, how dare you make such an exhibition of yourselves! Stop that ridiculous noise immediately! Do you have no notion of how to behave!"

"But Francis," I protested, "they've had a dreadful fright, poor little things! Chased by a bull!"

"It is highly unlikely that it was a bull," Francis said coldly. "It was more probably a cow. And, even if it had been, that is no excuse for such unbridled behavior."

I seem to remember we went home after that. I could hardly bring myself to speak to Francis and I told Peter fiercely that I thought it would be an absolute miracle if those two poor children ever grew up to be normal human beings with such a background. And I wondered now if they had. What warped emotions were hidden behind the facades of Mary's sullenness and Adrian's bleak passivity?

Adrian, certainly, was an unknown quantity. Since he'd grown up I don't believe I'd ever seen him except in his father's company, and then he was simply a cipher, speaking only when he was spoken to, looking at his father to see how he should react to any topic that might arise. Goodness knows what he was like on his own or with his friends—if, indeed, he had any friends. It seemed unlikely. He'd certainly reacted very strongly to his father's death, completely collapsing, perhaps because the prop he'd leaned upon all his life had been suddenly taken away from him.

I know Joan worried about him, even before the present crisis, and I'm sure he never talked to her. It seemed unlikely that he talked to anyone. But—a sudden thought struck me—perhaps Adrian had another life, kept secret from his family, especially his father. Perhaps there was something in that life that might have made it necessary for him to kill his father. I wondered if there was any way I could find out. Certainly he wouldn't confide in me. Perhaps Michael might be able to discover from Philip if there was more to Adrian than met the eye. And then there was Joan. I must say I found it hard to think about Joan without impatience. How any woman, especially in this day and age, could have put up with the sort of treatment she had from Francis was beyond my comprehension! Of course she'd been brought up by that horrible father to have an incredibly low opinion of herself, but still! I suppose I might just have to acknowledge that she was such a born doormat that she could accept the way Francis constantly denigrated all her opinions and activities, put her down in public, and generally treated her with contempt. What, as a mother myself, I couldn't understand was the way she allowed Francis to ruin the children's lives. I could see how she fretted for Mary and worried over Adrian, but even from the very earliest days of her marriage, before the pattern of Francis's treatment of them all had been set, she had (as far as I could tell) never protested at his behavior toward them, never even interceded on their behalf.

I thought how furious and frustrated I would have felt, how *anyone* would, for that matter, and how she must have bottled up her resentment for all those years. It wouldn't be surprising if something inside her had finally snapped and she had decided to free them all from the sort of slavery they had lived in for so long. Tomorrow I would talk to her, see if I could find out what she had been doing on the day that Francis died.

I was more wide awake than ever. I sat up in bed, put on the light and picked up my copy of *North and South* again. I read doggedly on for some time and gradually, soothed by the solid and familiar world of Mrs. Gaskell, I felt my lids grow heavy and slept at last.

# 14

When I'd phoned Joan to see if she'd be in the following morning she reminded me that it was market day, so I left the car in the main car park and, having pointed David in the direction of the police station, made my way through the busy streets toward the cathedral close. I love street markets and am sad that so many nowadays consist merely of stalls of cheap clothing and cut-price household goods. Culminster market, though, I'm glad to say, retains much of its original charm and you can buy fresh vegetables with the red soil still clinging to them, local cheeses, lardy bread and the sort of heavenly fudge that you can positively *feel* destroying your teeth and bumping up your cholesterol level!

I wandered happily among the stalls, set up in the shadow of the great cathedral as they must have been since medieval times, my shopping bag heavy with goodies. I paused at a stall piled high with balls and cones of wool, something I can never resist. The house is full of bags containing pieces of half-finished knitting. Not because I lack the application, but because there comes a time in the life of every attempted garment when it becomes too heavy to hold up in the air above the large, recumbent Siamese cat occupying his usual place in the evenings on my lap.

Nevertheless I found myself purchasing a quantity of clerical gray (the description coming readily to mind in these surroundings) wool to make a pullover for Michael and some very dashing cyclamen boucle from which I proposed to fashion a similar garment for myself.

The gray wool somehow reminded me of old Canon Burgess, perhaps because he had always worn a hand-knitted gray woollen cardigan, presumably not the same one all his life, but each identical in its grayness and shapelessness and presumably made for him by Evelyn. She had never married, but like so many of her generation kept house for her also unmarried brother. They were an eccentric pair, he absorbed in pastoral duties and, like Trollope's Septimus Harding, passionate about church music; she, even in her younger days, vague and absentminded, never quite in touch with the modern world, a characteristic made worse these days by increasing deafness. Still, she had managed to look after her brother in his recent illness and allowed him the privilege of dying with dignity in his own home. I knew Evelyn was one of the few people Joan felt at ease with. I suppose it was because Evelyn made no demands on her and, given her own inadequacies, never made her feel useless or incompetent. Still, it was good of Joan to have spent so many hours sitting in a sickroom, especially toward the end, when the invalid, sedated against the pain, was incapable of conversation. I was walking across the cathedral green now, and a thought came to me with such suddenness and such force that I felt obliged to sit down on the low stone wall that led to the entrance to the west cloisters.

With startling clarity, things fell into place. It had always been a puzzle how Francis's murderer had come by the means of killing him, morphine not being readily available to the general public, but I suddenly had a picture of Canon Burgess, sleeping perhaps, certainly unaware for most of the time what was going on around him. It was highly likely that he had been given morphine to alleviate the final stages of his illness and the picture in my mind now extended to include Joan abstracting some of the drug when Evelyn was out of the room. It would have been quite easy, especially since Evelyn was vague and confused and probably wouldn't have realized that any was missing. The three classic headings—means, the morphine; motive, years of misery with Francis and a belated wish to help her children; opportunity, Joan had the best opportunity of all, since she had made the sandwiches and taken them and the cake and (most important) the indigestion mixture across to the cathedral herself—they were all complete.

Having, as it were, established my case, I became aware that I was on my way to visit the person I was now certain was the murderer. She was also an old friend and, quite honestly, in spite of a natural reluctance to countenance the taking of human life, I couldn't find it in my heart, given the circumstances, to blame her. But it was certainly an awkward situation. Should I confront her with my suspicions?

I was now at the entrance to the deanery and the temptation to turn around and simply go away was very strong, but Joan, as ever on the lookout at the drawing-room window, was waving, so I reluctantly mounted the steps and went inside.

"It *is* nice to see you, Sheila," she said warmly. "Do come up."

While Joan poured the coffee we made general conversation and then she said, "Did you say that David was at the police station?"

"Yes," I replied, "the inspector wanted another word with him."

"Poor David, I'm so sorry he's having all this trouble."

"Well," I said, watching her carefully as I spoke, "he is their number one suspect. I mean, he was actually there when Francis ate or drank whatever it was that killed him."

Joan looked distressed. "But surely they don't think ..."

"They've got to suspect someone," I went on. "The poison didn't get there by itself, someone must have put it there."

"But still ..."

"And David did have a motive, a very strong one—money. It really must seem obvious to them."

Joan became very agitated. "But surely *you* don't think..."

"Oh no," I said, "I know David didn't kill Francis."

Joan was silent for a moment. She sat quite still, her eyes fixed beseechingly on me. Then she burst out, "Oh, it's all so dreadful! I don't think I can bear it!"

"Joan, what do you mean?"

She made a great effort and seemed to pull herself together. "I'm so worried about the children. Mary's so—I don't know, so different, hard and unsympathetic—not to me, don't think that—but saying such things about her father! And Adrian, he's so odd, withdrawn and peculiar. He doesn't say a word all through supper and then, immediately afterward, he goes straight to his room. And, Sheila, I've heard him in there *crying*, really sobbing, and I don't know what to do!"

She was standing up now, clasping her hands convulsively together. Her lips were compressed and she shook her head from side to side in agitation.

"Oh, Joan, my dear, I'm so sorry," I said helplessly. "I know it's been difficult for you all these years, but now you can lead your own life at last, make your own decisions ..."

She shook her head again, more vehemently.

"You don't *understand*," she cried, "you don't know what it's like for me to know that he's gone, that I'll never see him again! Oh Francis, Francis!"

She sank down onto the sofa and gave way to a fit of violent sobbing. After a while she burst out, "None of you understand—Mary's the same, I don't *want* things to be different, I just want him back. I love him so much, I've always loved him—he's been my life, all I've ever wanted! I don't think I can bear to go on without him!"

For a moment I stared at her in amazement, unable to take in what she was saying. For years we had all taken it for granted that Joan was the miserable downtrodden wife, longing to escape from a tyrannical husband. The simple fact that she was in love with him had never occurred to us. I crossed over to the sofa and sat beside her.

"My dear," I said gently, "I'm sorry, I've been crass and insensitive. Do forgive me."

Her sobbing quietened and she grasped my hand.

"It's all right," she said. "I know you were trying to be kind ...." She made an effort to collect herself. "I know you all found Francis difficult—he was, but that's because he had such high standards—for himself as well as for other people. He was such a splendid man, Sheila!"

I made some vague murmur of what I hoped she would take as assent. Joan took a handkerchief from the pocket of her cardigan and wiped her eyes. "When we first met and he seemed to be taking an interest in me I couldn't believe my luck! He was so brilliant and so handsome he could have married anybody! And, even then—well, I wasn't anything to write home about! I wasn't pretty or very bright—it seemed like a fairy tale!"

She looked at me, her eyes red and swollen with weeping, her face sallow without makeup, but, apart from the lines etched by age and anxiety, I could still see the young girl I had known many years ago, plain, eager to please, vulnerable.

"Yes, he was handsome, wasn't he—more so than David, really."

"He could have had anyone," she repeated. Then, looking at me with a rueful smile, she went on, "Of course I know he married me for the money and what my father could do for him. I wasn't naive enough, even then, to think that there could be any other reason. But I didn't care. I was grateful that there was something I could give him that he wanted and I tried to be a good wife to him and do all I could to help his career."

"You did so much!"

"I wasn't very good at things and I know he used to get impatient .... The children, too, he wanted so much for them, he had such plans. We were all such a disappointment to him—it was so unfair, we never lived up to his standards."

"You mustn't think that!" I protested.

"But I do—all the time. My life is so empty now, there's nothing left to live for!"

"Joan, please! You mustn't talk like that. You've got so much in your life—the children need you!"

"They don't, really. Well, perhaps Adrian does just now—though I don't seem able to get through to him at all. Of course I love them, but it's not the same." She laughed bitterly, without mirth. "Francis was the only thing that gave my life meaning. Even when he was angry or impatient—even..." She looked down, not meeting my eye. "Even when he went after someone else ...."

"You mean ...?"

"Oh yes," she said quietly, "he was unfaithful, there were other women in his life. Well, it's understandable, he was such an attractive man."

"But you never did anything about it?"

"What could I do? We couldn't afford any sort of scandal, it would have been so bad for his reputation—the bishop and everything. No, I never let him realize that I knew what was going on. You do see, don't you, I didn't dare say anything in case he'd found someone he really cared for, someone he'd risk *divorcing* me for! I would have lost him altogether then!"

"Oh Joan," I said helplessly.

"It only happened a couple of times," she assured me earnestly, "and he never even hinted that he might leave me!"

"Who were these women?" I asked curiously.

"One was the wife of the churchwarden when we were down in Cornwall; there was someone in London, I think, and recently there was someone down here, but I don't know who." She pulled her cardigan close about her and shivered. "What does it matter now? He's gone and I'll never see him again."

She was crying quietly now, the tears rolling unchecked down her face. Somehow this silent despair was more upsetting than the wild sobbing. I put my arm around her shoulders and we sat there for a while, neither of us saying anything.

So Francis had been having affairs, there could be a motive there. I wondered how I could find out who the mysterious woman in Culminster was. Perhaps Mary knew. If she did that might be another reason why she felt particularly bitter toward her father.

Joan made an effort to pull herself together. She mopped at her face with her handkerchief and stood up, almost composed.

"I'm so sorry, Sheila," she said. "I shouldn't have burdened you with my worries."

"My dear, I'm so glad you did."

"The children don't understand."

"It's always easier with one's own generation," I said soothingly.

"Yes. The young can't know .... They don't know how it feels—all those years together."

"I know," I said. "I felt like that when Peter died. When one of the pillars of the house you've built together is suddenly taken away. But," I said bracingly, "you have to go on. It's something you have to face up to. You must be strong."

She shook her head. "I don't know if I can. I've never been strong, you know that. How can I start now?"

I was silent, for how, indeed, could she start now. The sound of the doorbell shattered the silence.

"I expect that's David," I said. "He was going to meet me here."

Joan seemed to shrink back. "Oh dear," she said, "I don't think ..."

"You won't feel like seeing anyone, I'm sure," I said. "I'll tell him you're not very well, I'm sure he'll understand."

"Thank you, Sheila, that would be kind."

I gave her a quick hug and went downstairs to meet David.

I thought he was looking a little strained but I wanted to get him away from the deanery so I didn't ask him how he'd got on.

"Joan's a bit upset," I said. "She sent her love but didn't feel up to seeing anyone. Look, it's after twelve, why don't we have lunch here? There's a sort of tea shop place by the cathedral that does what they call light lunches. It's usually nice and quiet."

The Spinning Wheel (which really did have a spinning wheel in the window, along with the trays of homemade scones and maids of honor) was indeed quiet—we were the only customers and had our choice of gingham-covered tables. I led the way to one at the far end by the old fireplace, filled with a large arrangement of dried flowers and surrounded by a collection of horse brasses.

"Here, this will do."

After our food had arrived (quiche and salad for me, dish of the day: shepherd's pie for David) I said, "Poor Joan, she was very weepy—I'll tell you all about it in a minute. But first of all I want to know how you got on. What did the police want to see you about?"

David was making patterns with his fork in the mashed potato in front of him.

"It's all very odd," he said.

"What is?"

"Absolutely out of the blue!"

"*What?*"

"It's Nana. The police seem to think that she might have been murdered too."

# 15

I was absolutely stunned. I sat with my fork suspended in midair and stared at him.

"What on earth do you mean?"

He shrugged. "I think they've decided that I murdered poor old Nana to get the house empty and then did in Francis because he refused to sell."

"But she fell downstairs."

"They seem to think she might have been pushed."

"Oh, David, what rubbish," I exclaimed impatiently.

"Well, I suppose it makes sense to them."

"Hang on," I said, "when did she die?" I got out my diary. "You've probably got a perfectly good alibi for that day. Um, let me see, it was the twenty-first, wasn't it? Oh."

David looked at me quizzically. "Exactly," he said. "That was when you went to Exeter for the whole day with Rosemary and I simply stayed around the house. Actually, I went into Taviscombe in the morning, do you remember? To get those slug pellets you wanted. I passed the bottom of West Hill. I could easily have popped in and chucked the poor old dear down the stairs."

"But you couldn't have got in," I said. "You didn't have a key, did you?"

"No, but she'd have let me in. As the inspector made a point of saying, it would have been someone she knew and trusted."

"At that rate it might just as easily have been Francis."

"Francis," David pointed out patiently, "didn't have any reason to want the house empty."

"Well, there's absolutely nothing to indicate that you ever *did* go and see her," I said firmly, "so they can speculate all they like!"

"Actually ..." David was fiddling with the mashed potato again. "Actually there was."

"What do you mean?"

"Well, as a matter of fact, I did go and see Nana—not on that day, but a few days before."

I looked at him in surprise. "You never mentioned it."

"Well," he said, "it was a bit embarrassing. I went round there one morning to try and persuade her to move somewhere else. She was very vague. I mean, she knew who I was and so forth, but she kept thinking we were back in the past—you know, complaining about how untidy my room was and had I changed my vest. I tried to make her understand about things, but in the end I'm afraid I got a bit impatient with her and she was rather upset. I felt pretty mean then, you know, bullying the poor old thing like that, so I suppose I felt too ashamed to tell you I'd seen her."

"Oh dear," I said, "how sad. Still, the police aren't to know you'd been round. Unless someone saw you."

"No, it wasn't that. It's just that when I was round there I left behind a pair of gloves and they had my name in them."

"Why on earth did you have your name in your gloves?" I asked, sidetracked for a moment by this strange fact.

David laughed. "Nana's influence, would you believe. She always made us write our names on the lining of our gloves so that Francis and I didn't quarrel over whose pair was which. The habit's sort of stuck. Ironic, isn't it? I meant to go back and collect them when I realized they were missing, but then Nana died and, what with one thing and another, I forgot about them."

"How did the police know about the gloves? I mean, they didn't search the house when she died or anything. As far as anyone knew it was an accident, so there was no reason."

"No. But apparently the inspector suddenly had this thought about it possibly being murder, and, since the house hadn't been touched since she died, he got the key from Adrian and went to have a look around."

The waitress came and took away our plates, looking hurt at the amount of unconsumed food.

"Do you want a sweet?" she inquired. "There's apple pie or crumble."

David shook his head.

"No, thank you," I said, "just coffee."

"The trouble is," David said, "when they first asked me if I'd been to see Nana, I said I hadn't."

"Oh dear."

"Yes, well. Then Inspector Hosegood told me about the gloves and so I had to tell him what I've just told you. Which, in a way, made things worse."

"He'd think you'd been intimidating her?"

"Exactly. And then, when I couldn't bully her into moving, I lured her upstairs and pushed her down. Oh, *what* a tangled web we weave when first we practice to deceive!"

"Oh David, what a mess! Still"—I suddenly thought of something—"if you *had* done it, then surely you'd have been round straight away to collect your gloves—as soon as you knew they were missing!"

"We must hope the inspector has your quick wit, dear."

The waitress put two cups of very milky coffee before us.

"Did the inspector have anything else to say about Francis?" I asked. "Oh bother, can I borrow your sweeteners? I can't find mine in this stupid handbag. Thanks. Have they got any farther with that?"

"I don't think so. I did ask, but he was a bit noncommittal—well, he would be, I suppose, if he's got me cast as the murderer."

"Oh dear."

"So," David said, stirring his coffee vigorously, "how did you get on with Joan?"

"It was quite extraordinary," I replied. "I'd more or less decided she was the guilty party—she could easily have got hold of some morphine while she was sitting with old Canon Burgess, and the whole thing fitted perfectly. I was all set to try and confront her in some way, when she broke down."

"Goodness!"

"We got it all wrong, David—she was sobbing her heart out, she really loved him!"

"You're sure? It wasn't just an act—the grieving widow and all that?"

"Oh no, I'm quite sure. I know genuine grief when I see it. Poor Joan, she really does feel she hasn't anything left to live for!"

"Good God! I must say I find it hard to understand how anyone could grieve for a cold fish like Francis ..."

"And that's not all," I went on. "She told me that Francis had had several affairs, including a recent one with someone in Culminster!"

"You're joking! Francis!"

"So Joan said. Poor soul—she never dared to confront him for fear of losing him altogether."

"The slimy toad!" David said. "The sanctimonious bastard!"

"The thing is," I said, "it does spread the net a bit wider, as far as motives are concerned."

"You mean a jealous husband?"

"Perhaps. Or an extra motive for Mary or Adrian if they found out about it and felt as you do about his appalling hypocrisy, as well as being furious for their mother's sake."

David leaned back in his chair. "Well, I'm damned," he said. "Francis!"

"It's not so incredible from the female's point of view, I

suppose, whoever she is. I mean, *we* know what he was really like, but he was very good looking, and when he wanted to be—I mean, when he wanted something from somebody—he could be quite charming. Most of the females in the diocese doted on him—that sort of grand remoteness can be very attractive, if you fancy that kind of thing. No, I can easily see some poor, impressionable female being swept off her feet."

"I wonder who it was?"

I reached for my handbag and tried to catch the waitress's eye.

"I think I must have another chat with Mary, I have a feeling she may know more about all this than she's letting on." I sighed. "I just hope it doesn't mean that I've got to go riding again! Actually, it would certainly be easier to see her at the stables. Perhaps I'll go round on Saturday when she's likely to be there."

There was no one about when I entered the yard, though sounds of girlish laughter came from one of the stables followed by cries of "Mind what you're doing with that fork, Caroline, you ass!"

I approached the open door cautiously and put my head around. "Hello. Is Mary Beaumont anywhere around?"

A plump, pigtailed girl of about ten appeared. She was wearing jodhpurs, Wellington boots and a T-shirt that bore the proud legend CULMINSTER PONY CLUB, and was carrying a pitchfork.

"I'm frightfully sorry," she said politely, "she's not here. She had to take Rajah and Nelson down to the smith's. I don't think she'll be long. Fay's in the tack room, if you'd like to see her." She gestured toward a building at the end of the yard.

"Fine, thank you."

It might be interesting to have a word with Fay while I was waiting for Mary, I thought. I might pick up something there.

I knocked on the tack room door and went in and was immediately enveloped in a warm, cozy world smelling of horses and polish. It was an impressive room, with wooden walls where highly polished bridles hung on pegs, saddles on stands and a great many rosettes that spoke eloquently of success in innumerable shows. Fay was sitting on a stool polishing a bit.

"Hello," she said, "I know you, don't I?"

"I'm Sheila Malory, a friend of Mary's."

"Yes, of course, I remember. You went out on Prudence, didn't you? Do you want to book another ride?"

"No—well, not at the moment. I just wanted to have a word with Mary."

"She's taken a couple of horses to be shod," Fay said, "but she won't be long if you'd like to wait. Here, chuck the stuff off that chair and sit down."

"Do forgive me intruding like this, but the girl in one of the stables said you were in here."

"Jennifer? Yes, she and her friend Caroline seem to ask nothing more of life than to spend their weekends mucking out here."

"Little girls and horses," I said smiling.

"Absolutely! Thank God for child labor. You ought to see this place in the school holidays!"

"As I said, I'm sorry to barge in like this, but I wanted to have a word with Mary about her mother—I'm very worried about her—and so I couldn't very well go to the deanery."

"I understand. How is Mrs. Beaumont? Mary hasn't said much about how things are at home since ..."

"I think it's all a bit fraught. Her mother's very upset, of course, and her brother seems to have broken down completely. Mary is the only strong one now."

"Yes, she's always been pretty tough underneath. Not quite tough enough to stand up to that terrible father of hers, though—I'm sorry," Fay broke off and looked at me inquiringly. "I know the Beaumonts have been friends of yours for some time ..."

"You can say what you like about Francis," I said. "He wasn't exactly one of my favorite people. No, it's Joan I'm concerned about. She adored him, strange as it may seem, and she's going to need an awful lot of support from Mary, since it looks as though Adrian's going to be no help at all."

Fay laid down the bit and took a bridle off one of the pegs and began to work on it. "It sounds a dreadful thing to say, given the circumstances of her father's death, but Mary's been a different girl since all this happened."

"I know she's always wanted to work here," I said, "so now perhaps she can."

"Not just work," Fay said. "She knows I've been looking for a partner in the business and she thinks that now her mother can get at her own money at last she may be able to come in with me. Actually, the timing's right. I've just had an offer from another friend, a girl I used to work with at the Priory Riding Center a couple of years ago. She's quite keen to come in with me. Of course, I've more or less given Mary first refusal, so, as I say ..."

"I see. Well, I do hope things work out for Mary. She's had a pretty dismal life up to now."

There was a clatter of horses' hooves in the yard outside.

"That'll be Mary back again," Fay said. She put her head around the door and called out, "Mary! A visitor for you! Why don't you both go into the office and make yourselves a cup of coffee. You haven't got another lesson until twelve-thirty."

I waited until Mary had seen to the horses and then followed her into the office. Unlike the tack room, where everything was neat and well ordered, the office was chaotic, with papers scattered about, mixed up with bits of harness, polishing cloths and old copies of *Horse and Hound*.

Mary pushed a clutter of brushes and curry combs to one side and plugged in the electric kettle.

"Nice to see you, Sheila," she said. "Have you come to book a ride?"

"No," I said hastily, "I mean, I'd love to some other time but I'm a bit tied up just now, with David staying and everything. As I said to Fay, I'm sorry to bother you here, but I did want to have a word with you about your mother. I'm really worried about her, she still seemed to be in a terrible state when I saw her yesterday. I'm afraid she misses your father dreadfully."

Mary still had her back to me, as she spooned coffee into a couple of mugs, so I couldn't see her face. "Yes," she said, "I do find that hard to understand, when you'd think she'd be as glad to be rid of him as I was."

"Well," I replied, rather flustered at this plain speaking, "I'm afraid she isn't. The fact is she was still very much in love with him."

Mary turned and handed me a mug of coffee. "Hard to imagine," she said. "How could she be?"

"Love is like that," I said rather tritely, "there's no rhyme or reason in it. She says she feels there's nothing left to live for."

"For heaven's sake!" Mary exclaimed impatiently. "I've made plans for us all—it's going to be great!"

"You mean buying a partnership with Fay?" I asked. "I know Joan would want to help you with that—she said something about wishing she could do it, ages ago, before your father died."

"Yes, she's got some sort of trust—there's quite a bit of money in it, I believe—though Father would never let her have anything to do with it while he was alive."

"It would be marvelous if you could buy a partnership here," I said. "I'm sure it's a very flourishing business and it's so much the sort of thing you should be doing—you're a splendid teacher!"

Mary flushed with pleasure. "It's what I've always, always

wanted," she said vehemently. "It *is* a good business, even as it is, but Fay wants to expand and do special courses, dressage, eventing and things like that."

"It all sounds very exciting," I said, "and how marvelous that you're able to come up with the money just now! I gather Fay's had an offer from some other girl ..."

Mary flushed again, this time with anger. "That Sally Ross! Coming here all the time, trying to butter Fay up! She's got masses of money—her father's rolling! But she doesn't know anything about horses or running a place like this—it would be just a hobby with her, just an excuse to hang round Fay!"

"Fay did say that she'd given you first refusal," I said soothingly.

"Yes, well, she knows that I'd work like a slave to make this place successful."

"I'm sure she does." I took a sip of my coffee, which was very strong and rather bitter, and wondered why other people's coffee was never quite like one's own. "She'd be an idiot not to realize what a tremendous asset you'd be, and I'm sure Fay's not an idiot!"

"She really is terrific," Mary said earnestly, "she's built all this up from nothing in just a couple of years. She's a brilliant rider—she could have been up to Olympic standard but she didn't have the money behind her—and marvelous at organization, too. It really is wonderful working with her. I'm moving in here soon. I'm not sure when, it depends on Mother and how soon we have to get out of the deanery—I'll have to be there to help her with that."

"Well, if there's anything I can do there, please let me know," I said. "You said something about her buying a cottage near here. Is that settled?"

"Well, it depends on probate and things like that. I suppose Father will have left Mother well provided for—he knew all about money!"

"I imagine all that will take some time. Where will Joan and Adrian live until then?"

"Mother did say something about staying with Evelyn Burgess for a bit. And I suppose Adrian might move in with his girlfriend."

"His *what*?"

"Oh, Adrian's got a girlfriend, though he's had to keep it a deadly secret because of Father."

"But why?"

Mary shrugged. "I don't know. Because she was what Father would call 'unsuitable,' I suppose."

"Do you know who she is?" I asked.

"Haven't the faintest." Mary sloshed some more water from the kettle into her mug. "Adrian never confides in me. But there's been the odd phone call when he was out—you know, a female voice, wouldn't leave a message. Anyway, Myra Lewis, who lives in Stoke Courcy, has seen them together several times in a pub there."

"Good Heavens!" I said. "But then"—I thought of something—"you'd think he'd be—well, not pleased exactly, but relieved that he can meet this girl quite openly now that your father's dead."

"Instead of which," Mary said slowly, "he's gone to pieces. Odd. I hadn't thought of that."

"Do you think your mother knows about it?" I asked.

"She hasn't said anything. I shouldn't think so. Adrian wouldn't have told her about it in case she let it out to Father. She isn't very good at keeping secrets."

"She kept one, though," I said.

Mary looked at me inquiringly.

"She never let Francis know that she'd found out about his affairs."

Mary gave a short, bitter laugh. "Oh, that!" she said. "I'm pretty sure he did know and despised her even more for not confronting him with them."

"She was so frightened of losing him," I said sadly. "So you knew about it too. She told me there had been several—someone in Culminster, even. Do you know who it was?"

"Yes, I do, as a matter of fact, though I never told Mother. There was a letter. Father must have dropped it in the passage outside his study. I picked it up and looked to see what it was. I got quite a surprise! It was from a woman called Judy, begging him to go and see her—a really emotional letter—apparently he'd ended their affair and she was desperate to see him. I could hardly believe it. Father, of all people! All that hypocrisy on top of everything else—it made me hate him even more."

"And she lived in Culminster?" I inquired tentatively.

"The address at the top of the letter was Rose Cottage, Shircombe."

"Shircombe? Oh, I know, it's that rather pretty village on the Taunton Road. What did you do with the letter? I don't imagine you mentioned it to your father?"

"What do you think! No, I put it on his desk among some other papers. I don't suppose he even knew he'd dropped it."

"When was this?" I asked.

"Oh, a while back. A couple of years ago—three, maybe. Why?"

"Oh, nothing. I just wondered if perhaps it might have been the motive—you know ..."

"You mean a woman spurned and all that?"

"Yes, well, that, or a jealous husband, if she was married... But not if it happened that long ago."

"No, I suppose not."

We sat in silence for a while and then I asked, "Have you heard anything else from the police?"

"No, not really. Oh, yes, Mother was going to ring you up—they've released the body. The funeral's next week. The bishop's officiating, the full works in the cathedral, and

Mother hopes that you and Uncle David will come. I expect she'll ring you about it."

"Yes, of course. It will be easier for everyone when that's over."

"When he's safely underground," Mary said vindictively, "but even then he'll still be making his influence felt, making life miserable for everyone, just like he did in his lifetime!"

# 16

Goodness, that girl is bitter!" I said to David and Michael that evening. "She really hated her father."

"Well, he wasn't exactly good parent material," Michael said. "Not what you'd call loving and caring. So do you think she hated him enough to do him in?"

"She had a very strong motive," I replied, "apart from the hating. It seems that it was her last chance to go in with Fay in the stables. She was obviously very jealous of this other woman—Sally something—who'd made an offer. A bit of rivalry there, and not just on the business side, I gather."

"Green-eyed monster?" Michael inquired.

"It looks like it, yes. Anyway, it was something that she *really* wanted, something that I think she'd be quite ruthless about. There really is quite a lot of Francis in Mary, more than one realized!"

"Well, she was around in that part of the cathedral when I was with Francis," David said, "so I suppose she could have popped in before we arrived and put the fatal potion in his medicine glass. Very nasty, though, to think of such unbridled family passions—like the worst excesses of Jacobean drama, it'll be poisoned gloves next!"

"Well, *someone* killed Francis," I said, "and I believe almost all poisonings are done by a member of the victim's family."

"Anyway," Michael said, "she could probably have put the stuff into the medicine glass at home."

"Before Joan took the tray over, you mean? Yes, I'm sure Mary always had lunch at the deanery, so she'd have been on the spot, as it were. Also," I continued, "there's another thing she told me. She'd found out about Francis's affair with this woman in Culminster—well, not exactly Culminster, Shircombe, actually. Someone called Judy. Mary was pretty upset about that, too—it all adds up."

"Are you going to tell your inspector friend?" Michael asked. "After all, if it's going to divert his beady eye from David here, then I certainly think you should."

"It seems a bit mean ..." David said reluctantly.

"This is no time for chivalry," I said firmly. "Actually, I'd like to see if I can find out a bit more about this Judy person. I know Mary said the affair was over several years ago, but you never know—these things send out ripples."

"I can't imagine how you intend to go about it," David said. "I mean, you can hardly go knocking on people's doors on the off chance!"

"Ah, but I've got an address," I said smugly. "Rose Cottage. All I need now is a pretext."

"And I'm sure that will present *no* problems to you, dear," David said sweetly. "I begin to pity the poor woman. Just think—an affair with Francis *(how* the spirit sinks at the thought) and then pursued by the Eumenides in the shape of Sheila Malory, girl detective! What a busy day you've had!"

"That's not all," I said. "Mary told me that she's pretty sure Adrian has a girlfriend."

They both turned and looked at me in amazement.

"And one, moreover," I continued, "that he apparently found it necessary to keep secret from his family."

"Why?" Michael asked.

"Your guess is as good as mine, but Mary seemed to think it was because she was unsuitable in some way.

"Francis was a dreadful snob," David said, "so that widens the field of his disapproval considerably."

"They meet in secret in a pub in Stoke Courcy, so Mary's been told. Of course!" I exclaimed. "We could all go there for a drink one evening and see if we can spot them."

"*No*, Ma," Michael said. "Count me out! I am not going to hang around some dismal alehouse in Stoke Courcy (which is one of the dreariest villages in the whole of West Somerset) on the off chance of surprising Adrian and his lady friend. It would be boring if he didn't turn up and embarrassing if he did! Take David, if you like. Being a thespian, he could probably disguise himself as a pot man or something and carry the whole thing off with aplomb, whatever that may be."

David groaned. "The whole concept sounds pretty fraught to me."

"Spoilsports!" I said. "Oh well, it was just an idea. I'll keep it in reserve if the Judy female is a dead end."

I was standing, staring in the window of our one and only dress shop at a jacket and skirt in a particularly trying shade of mustard and wondering who on earth would be prepared to pay £275 for the doubtful privilege of wearing it, when a voice behind me said, "Goodness, Estelle's prices get more and more astronomical! It's just as well that she never has anything now that one would be seen dead in!" It was my friend Rosemary.

"I know," I said, "just look at this monstrosity and that dress there in a really horrendous shade of green—it would make you look like one of the undead!"

Rosemary laughed. "Have you got time for a coffee? I've only just got away from Mother's—she's having one of her maddeningly slow days when everything she wants me to do takes twice as long to explain. I really need a little breather before I go and wrestle with the bank—she's convinced that they've forgotten all her standing orders and I've got to go and remonstrate with them. Of course, it'll turn out that she never instructed them in the first place and I'll feel an absolute fool ..."

Over coffee and Danish pastries ("Honestly, the amount of comfort eating I have to do after every session with Mother...") I gave Rosemary an account of my meeting with Mary.

"I began by feeling sorry for her," I said, "but now it's Joan I'm unhappy about. I don't think she knows what she wants yet, she's still in a state of shock. I suppose the young don't see that as you get older it takes longer and longer to adjust to things."

"I think she'd be better off with Evelyn Burgess permanently," Rosemary said, "if it could be arranged. Evelyn's a gentle soul, even if she is a bit eccentric, and they've always got on well together."

"And then Adrian could go and live with his girlfriend—that is, if he ever succeeds in pulling himself together."

"My goodness, yes, that *was* a surprise! I'd no idea. Still, he's back at work. Jack had to ring his firm about something the other day and he got Adrian. He said he sounded even more feeble than usual. But, then, you know Jack, he never did suffer fools gladly. Oh yes, and talking of fools, do you know what Sybil's done now? The idiotic woman only told me yesterday that she's off to *Finland* (such an extraordinary place to go for a holiday!) tomorrow so she won't be around for the St. John's flag day. So now I'm a collector short."

Rosemary mopped up the remaining crumbs of icing on her plate with her finger and looked at me speculatively. "I don't suppose ..." she inquired. "No, forget it—you've got enough to do with all those Beaumonts and David staying for goodness knows how long."

"Oh, he's no trouble," I said, "and very entertaining company. I shall miss him when he goes back."

"Which will be when?"

"When it's all over, I suppose, and the police don't feel they need him under their eye. Oh, did I tell you, the police asked for an adjournment of the inquest, so he'll have to stay for that at least." I finished the last of my coffee. "Oh, go on, then, I'll fill in for Sybil on Saturday. Where's her usual pitch?"

"Outside Woolworth's—it's quite good, there are usually lots of people in and out. Bless you, that *is* a weight off my mind. Would you mind coming round to the committee rooms now and getting the collecting tin and the flags? Oh, and this year we're hoping that people will do a bit of door-to-door collecting before Saturday as well. I know it's a bore to do, but we did it last year and the takings went up quite a bit. People seem to give more generously on their own doorsteps—shame and embarrassment, I suppose. Would you mind?"

An idea came to me. "No," I said, "I don't mind. Actually, I think it's a splendid plan."

Shircombe has become little more than a dormitory village to Culminster. You can tell that by the way almost all the houses have been gentrified within an inch of their lives, crouching under fancy chocolate-box-style thatch and festooned with hanging baskets. Although it was a weekday, there were still several Range Rovers parked on newly graveled driveways, presumably for the wives-at-home to do the supermarket shopping and the school run.

It was one of those rare, boiling hot summer days when the car turns into a greenhouse and I was conscious of being sticky, crumpled and uncomfortable when I parked by the village green (a rustic seat, ducks on a meticulously kept pond) and got out and looked around the center of the village. There were Myrtle and Woodbine and Pear Tree cottages, but no Rose. Fortunately there was a village shop. Inside I was not really surprised to see tins of lobster bisque, jars of cherries in kirsch and a display of Bath Olivers. The man behind the counter, palpably a brisk, newly retired ex-naval type escaping from the rat race, greeted me pleasantly. I bought a jar of Kalamata olives and asked if he could tell me where Rose Cottage was.

"Mrs. Fletcher's? Oh, that's a little way out of the village. You go up past the church and there's a lane to the right. Rose Cottage is the first house on the left."

"Thank you so much." I looked around and said appreciatively, "I must say you do have a splendid stock of unusual things."

He smiled ruefully. "People in the village get most of their stuff from the supermarkets in Culminster, so we have to cater for more specialist demands if we're going to survive."

"What do the old villagers think of"—I picked up a tin and examined the label—"Balti Stir-Fry Sauce?"

"There aren't many old villagers left and the ones there are only come in for the post office, to get their pensions. There's still one bus a week into Culminster and they all go and stock up at Tesco."

"Village life in the 'nineties," I said.

"Well, to be honest, it isn't really what my wife and I expected. But you've got to adapt, haven't you?"

"Yes," I said sadly, "I suppose you have."

I turned the car and drove up the lane. Rose Cottage stood alone. Unlike the cottages in the village, it was not picturesque, being a worker's dwelling put up as economically as possible to house some nineteenth-century agricultural laborer. It was built of gray stone with a slate roof and, although some attempt had been made to soften its ungracious outline with climbing roses and a honeysuckle, it still remained uncompromisingly utilitarian. There was a small garden, predominantly yellow and orange, planted with marigolds and nasturtiums, presumably grown from seed.

There was a little lay-by just beyond the cottage and I parked there. I pinned my collector's badge to my frock, got out the collecting tin and tray of flags and walked up the short path to the house.

There was no answer to my ring and I wondered if I had had a wasted journey. It was very quiet and only the buzzing of industrious bees plunging in and out of the honeysuckle broke the stillness. I rang again and this time I heard some movement inside the house. The door was opened by a woman in her late thirties, tall and slim, with dark curly hair and a pleasant expression. In her arms she carried a small child.

"Hello," she said, "can I help you?"

I stood transfixed, unable to speak. The child bore an extraordinary resemblance to Francis.

# 17

For a moment the image of the woman and child swam before my eyes and I put up my hand as if to brush it away. I heard the woman ask, "Are you all right?" Her voice was kind and concerned.

I made an effort to pull myself together and said, "I'm so sorry. It's rather a hot day ..."

"Look," she said, "come in and sit down for a moment."

She led the way through a tiny hall into a small, low-ceilinged sitting room, pleasantly cool after the heat of the day outside.

"Do sit down," she said, "and I'll get you a glass of water." I put my collecting tin and tray on the floor and sat down obediently on the sofa, feeling rather guilty in the face of this kindness, when my eye was caught by a photograph on the small table beside the sofa. It was a framed snapshot of a smiling group—the woman, the child and Adrian Beaumont.

With an increasing sense of unreality I picked up the photograph and was staring at it in amazement when the woman came back into the room. She stopped short in the doorway when she saw me with the photograph in my hand. She put down the glass of water she was carrying and said brusquely, "What are you doing?"

I took a deep breath. "I'm sorry," I said, "it must seem very rude of me, but—well, it's the most extraordinary coincidence. My name is Sheila Malory, I'm a friend of the Beaumonts, you see."

"I see."

As if sensing the feeling of tension in the air, the child began to cry.

"It's all right, Robbie," she said soothingly, "it's all right."

She sat down in the chair opposite to me and cuddled him on her lap until he was quiet again. Now as I looked at the child more closely I realized that he was hardly more than a baby, scarcely a year old. Yet her liaison with Francis had ended three years ago. And then there was the photograph. An incredible idea began to take shape in my mind as I sat in silence watching the woman rocking her child.

After a while she spoke. "You said you were a friend of the Beaumonts."

"Yes. I've known Francis and David all my life and I'm devoted to David—but, well, Francis and I never got along. I'm very fond of Joan, though, and Mary and Adrian ..." My voice trailed away, my gaze strayed once more to the photograph and I found myself asking, "Is that Adrian's child?"

"Yes, Robert is Adrian's son."

"I was confused for a moment," I said, "because he looks so very like Francis."

"Yes."

Again we sat in silence and then I said, "Do you mind if I have that glass of water? I really do feel a little peculiar."

"Yes, of course," she said politely, as if this was an ordinary social visit.

I drank a little of the water and began to feel more myself.

"Look," I said suddenly, "you must think I'm just being nosy and gossipy, but I've been so involved with the family since Francis's murder—David and I were there the day it happened, you see, and David's staying with me—as I said, we're old friends. I've been trying to do what I can to help Joan and Mary, and, well, we've all been *dreadfully* worried about Adrian ... If you could help us with him in any way we'd all be so grateful."

She shook her head. "I haven't seen him since his father died," she said, "and he won't speak to me on the phone. I don't know what to do."

"We none of us knew about you," I said helplessly, "we had no idea—about the baby and everything. In fact, Mary thought ..." I caught myself up quickly, but not quickly enough.

"She thought that I was having an affair with her father?"

"Well, yes, yes, she did. She found a letter."

"And that is why you're here today?"

I felt the blood rush into my face. "Yes. I'm sorry."

She smiled. "It was very enterprising of you."

"I just wanted to find out more about Francis—because of the murder, you see. I mean, the police suspect David, which is ridiculous ..."

"So you thought you'd see if you could find another suspect?"

"Well, not exactly ... perhaps."

"In that case, I'd better tell you all about it from the beginning."

The little boy was asleep now and she got up gently and put him down on the quilt in a playpen in the corner of the room. "I'll make a cup of tea," she said. "That's always supposed to be the suitable thing to do on every occasion, isn't it?"

"My name is Judy Fletcher," she said, when she had poured the tea and we were sitting, almost cozily, together, "but I expect you already know that." She looked at me inquiringly and I nodded.

"And, yes, I did have an affair with Francis Beaumont. I'm a computer programmer and he wanted some work done—to do with the cathedral finances—and someone recommended me. I work from home and he used to come here quite often to check the progress of the programs or to amend them. He was, oh I don't know, different, I suppose, from anyone else I'd ever met. That *absolute* certainty about everything! I'd just divorced my husband—he was weak and useless, in practically every way, feeble! It was the usual story. *He* found someone who wasn't pushing and organizing him all the time and went off and left me. It was a relief when he'd gone, actually, and when Francis appeared—everything that Clive (that's my husband) was not—well! I fell for him quite heavily."

She reached into the pocket of her skirt and produced some cigarettes. "Do you?" I shook my head. "Do you mind if I do? I know I shouldn't with Robert around, but there are times ..."

I smiled sympathetically and she lit the cigarette and inhaled deeply. "Where was I? Oh yes, Francis. He could be very charming when he wanted. I was flattered, of course, and I think he found it good for his self-esteem to know that someone so much younger found him attractive."

"I can imagine," I said drily.

"It lasted for about six months," Judy said. "On his side, at least. When he said it was all over I wouldn't accept it—I made scenes, threatened to tell his wife, all that sort of thing."

"How did he cope with that?" I asked curiously.

She laughed. "He offered me money. That was Francis's solution to every problem."

I put my empty cup on the tray. "So what did you do?" She shrugged. "I came to my senses. The very fact that he thought he could buy me off opened my eyes to what sort of person he was. So I thought, yes, all right, I'll take your money, I'll get something out of it."

"Good for you!" I said approvingly.

"That's how I met Adrian. Francis couldn't just write a check, not for any substantial sum of money. There'd have been problems with various accounts—I don't understand the details. Anyway, it was arranged that Adrian should bring me installments of cash, every month. He didn't know about his father and me, he was supposed to think it was payment for computer work I'd done."

"Neat," I said.

"Oh yes, Francis was devious, all right."

"So how did it happen? You and Adrian?"

She smiled. "Poor lamb, I felt sorry for him the moment I saw him. I knew at once what sort of person he was. Not weak and blustering like Clive, but weak and helpless, a sweet-natured person who'd never been given any sort of affection. It was heartbreaking."

"Yes," I said. "Joan, his mother, did try, but Francis always accused her of making him soft, as he said, and Joan was completely under his thumb!"

"Adrian was too. So I decided, that was my first instinct, that I was going to undermine that domination. Afterward, of course, I grew fond of Adrian for himself, but my first impulse was to revenge myself on Francis by destroying his influence with his son." She stubbed out her cigarette with some violence. "I began by telling him about my affair with Francis. That shook him, I can tell you. And then I told him how his father had dropped me and then paid me off. He was very upset. By then, he'd been coming to see me quite frequently, not just to bring the money. I'd made him welcome, tried to build up his confidence in himself, given him some sort of affection. He fell in love with me, bless him. He'd never been in love with anyone before. It was very touching, and I grew very fond of him. No, I'm not in love with him, but I do love him dearly."

Her expression softened and she glanced toward the playpen and the sleeping child.

"And the baby?" I asked.

"Clive and I never had any children—he couldn't—I suppose I might have tried to make something of the marriage if we had. And a child, of course, was the last thing Francis would have wanted, but I ... I suddenly realized that I wanted a child. I was nearly forty years old and it was my last chance. I suppose you could say I used Adrian. Used him to get my revenge on Francis, used him to father a child."

"How did Adrian feel about it? The baby, I mean?"

"Oh, he was so thrilled!" She picked up the photograph of them all together and smiled lovingly.

"So why did you both keep all this a secret?" I asked.

"You know Adrian. You know how frightened he is of his father, how he could never make a move without his approval. He'd been stressed enough about our being together, and I knew that if I tried to push him into acknowledging our relationship, then he'd be right over the edge, and I couldn't do that to him."

"Yes, I see. But what I don't see," I went on, "is why, now that Francis is dead, Adrian is behaving in this extraordinary way. I mean, you'd think he'd be delighted to come out into the open ..."

"I'm really worried about him. I honestly don't know what to do." She took another cigarette from the packet and lit it. "Have you seen him since his father died?"

"No, I haven't. When I went to the deanery just after—you know—Adrian was in his room and, according to Joan, he wouldn't come out for several days. He was in a pretty bad state. I think he must be a little better now, I believe he's back at work. But I did see him just before his father died and I thought he looked rather ill then."

"Yes, he's been in a strange sort of state for several months now. When he came here he was terribly tense and anxious, and then, gradually, he'd relax and seem to enjoy being with us, just like he used to. But, when he had to go, the tension would come back. He wouldn't tell me what was upsetting him, but I knew there was something. I did try to take his mind off things. I got a sitter and we went out to the pub a couple of times. But he was always nervous and jumpy if we were out together, afraid that someone might see us together."

"I can imagine."

We sat quietly for a while and then I asked, "Would you marry Adrian, now that it would be possible?"

She shook her head. "No, I couldn't do that."

"Not even for Robert?"

"No. I'm so much older than he is—though that's not the reason. I don't particularly want to be married. I've got what I want. I've got Robert. Of course, I'd always let Adrian be involved, if that's what he wanted, but Robert is my child. I made that quite clear from the beginning. I support him myself from what I earn—I've never taken any money from Adrian, for Robert or for me, and I never would."

There was a small cry from the child in the playpen and she went over and picked him up.

"He's hungry," she said.

Robert, now awake, regarded me over his mother's shoulder with wide eyes.

"He's beautiful," I said, smiling at him. "He's going to look exactly like Francis used to look when he was a child. It's funny, one never saw how like his father Adrian looked—I suppose it's because he was always in Francis's shadow and one never noticed. But," I said, picking up the photograph again, "the resemblance here is very strong." I turned again to look at Judy. "Please forgive me for coming like this. As you must know, it's all a bit difficult at the moment. The police haven't actually accused anyone of Francis's murder but it's obvious they are concentrating on David, who, I must admit, did have a motive to wish his brother dead. But I've known David for years and there's no way he could kill anyone."

"So who do you think did it?" Judy asked.

"I honestly don't know."

"It could have been me," she said, "several years ago.

When he rejected me and I hated him. But now ... I won't say I'm sorry Francis is dead, not after the way he treated me and the way he's ruined Adrian's life, but I didn't kill him." She looked directly at me. "Do you believe me?"

"Oh yes," I said, "I believe you." I picked up my tray and collecting tin. "I must go, I'm sorry ..."

"No. It's been a relief, in a way, to be able to talk to someone." She put the child down, holding onto his hand. "Look, could you do something for me?"

"Of course. What is it?"

"Could you try and see Adrian? Could you, please, ask him to come and see me? Or even telephone. Anything. Please let him know how worried I am. Will you do that?"

"Yes," I said, "yes, I will."

"And you'll let me know how he is?"

"Of course." I bent down to the child. "Good-bye, Robert."

In a sudden access of shyness, the child buried his face in his mother's skirt. She smiled.

"Good-bye. Come and see us again, if you're ever this way."

At the gate I turned to wave and they both waved back, Judy waving Robert's hand for him and Robert laughing.

As I got into the car, now hotter than ever from standing in the blazing sun, I thought that although I was quite sure that Judy hadn't murdered Francis, I was equally certain that she and Robert had provided Adrian with a very good motive for doing so.

# 18

Darling, you look absolutely terrible. What *have* you been doing?"

David's expression of concern, when I got home, indicated that I looked as exhausted as I felt.

"It has been a bit of a day!" I said, flopping down in a chair.

"Would you like a delicious cup of tea, or do you think something more stimulating is in order? The sun is, to all intents and purposes, over the yardarm."

"Oh, yes. Just a little gin and a great deal of tonic please, and have one yourself else I'll feel guilty!"

While David poured the drinks I told him about my afternoon with Judy.

"It was a bit of a brass *neck* calling on her like that," he said. "I do think enterprise like that deserves some reward, but one could hardly have hoped for such riches!"

"I know. I was absolutely staggered. Adrian, of all people!

Still, you do see, it does give him a very strong motive for killing his father. I mean, not just being terrified that Francis would find out about Judy and the baby—and you can imagine what hell he'd have made life for all of them!—but also anger about the way Judy had been treated."

"Mm. Poor lad. I must say I'm so sorry for him, he was used by everyone. Taken over by his father, used by this Judy female ..."

"But," I said quickly, "she's also given him the only real happiness he's ever known."

"I suppose. So, what are you going to do?"

"Oh dear," I sighed, "it's very difficult. I promised I'd see Adrian so I must try. But, you see, if he did kill Francis that would explain his extraordinary behavior. He loves Judy and the child so much that he'd want to keep right away from them in case *they* might be suspected or involved in any way."

"Not to mention," David said, "providing a motive."

"Exactly. And I was so touched by that little family—you should have seen that photo, it was really sweet—I'd hate to see it all destroyed."

"Such a *complicated* family tangle," David mused, "like an early play by Anouilh. Quite extraordinary!"

"What's extraordinary?" Michael asked, coming into the sitting room. "Hullo, are you two at the gin already!"

"Oh goodness," I exclaimed, "you're home early! I haven't *started* supper yet!"

"I had to go and see an old gent in West Lodge, about his will," Michael said defensively, "and it didn't seem worth going back to the office."

I got to my feet. "You have a drink with David and he'll tell you all about what I've found out, and I'll start cooking!"

All through supper we talked around and around the discoveries I'd made, about Adrian and Judy and about Mary and her plans for the stables.

"Well," Michael said, "it could be either of them. Assuming, of course, that Adrian was around that lunchtime and able to slip the dope into his father's medicine."

"Or," I reminded him, "he could have gone into Francis's room in the cathedral while Monica was away sorting out the flower problem."

"Anyway," David asked, "how are you going to get to see him? He's been very elusive up to now."

"I don't know, I'll see how things go ..."

"My money's on Mary," Michael said. "She sounds much more efficient than the wretched Adrian."

"Yes, but I get the feeling that Adrian was more desperate." I poured myself a glass of water. "Now can we stop talking about it? I do feel I've had quite enough of all this for one day!"

"What you need is a nice restful day in the sun," Michael said. "I've got a day's leave and I was going to take it tomorrow to go to the cricket. Come with me—you know you enjoy it."

"Oh, darling, tomorrow? I'm sure I was supposed to be doing something ..."

"Then don't. How about you, David? Will you come too?"

"That's very sweet of you, Michael, but I'm not, actually, *into* cricket. I love Wimbledon—well, the *idea* of Wimbledon, though I usually go to sleep when I watch it on the telly—but I'm not really *sportif*."

"I thought there was a very strong link between the theater and cricket," I said. "Think of those charity matches they always seem to be playing. Oh, and what about Frank Benson and his famous cricket team?"

"Frank Benson?" Michael inquired.

"A famous Edwardian actor-manager, you ignorant child, based at Stratford. There's that heavenly painting of him, you know the one, David, all noble Roman profile and wearing shorts and a blazer!"

"It was Benson," David said, "who advertised for 'a personable young man to play Laertes, must be a good medium-paced bowler.' "

"That would make rather a good game," Michael said. "Claudius, I think, would bowl nasty little leg-breaks, and Hamlet? He was probably a batsman, some gentlemanly stroke play, a bit of a David Gower."

I do enjoy a day at the Taunton ground. Michael is a vice

president, which sounds quite grand but only means that you pay a slightly larger subscription than the ordinary members. As we climbed up the steps of the Old Pavilion, Michael said with satisfaction, "Oh good, our usual seats are free."

The usual seats are directly behind the wicket and, as such, much sought after, which is why Michael insisted on our leaving home practically at the crack of dawn. Not that the actual seats themselves are anything to write home about, being old cinema seats that have seen better days. However, old habitués bring cushions to ease the situation and I always have a heavy woollen rug, since even on the hottest day there is always a stiff breeze, coming from goodness knows where, that chills the extremities.

I settled the picnic bag at my feet and got out the binoculars. It's not that I don't enjoy the actual cricket, but I must admit that I derive equal pleasure from scanning the players' balcony, seeing who's chatting to whom, who's reading *The Mirror*, who's having a late breakfast of meat pasty and Pepsi. A slight movement in the row behind and a familiar voice indicated that I would be able to indulge my other pleasure. People at the county ground (like Michael and me) like to sit in the same seats every time and we quite often have behind us two elderly men, both of whom talk nonstop throughout the day. Mostly they talk about the game (very knowledgeably, since one of them wears an MCC tie and the other appears to have been at one time captain of an amateur team in North London) but often they talk about the minutiae of their lives or comment on current events. Michael calls them The Wiseacres and he rolled his eyes at me in mock horror when he heard their voices. But I was delighted, since I look upon them as a sort of living soap opera and long to hear how Dora (MCC's wife) is managing with her broken arm and if North London's brother-in-law has made a go of his home improvements.

It was a good game. Somerset took a satisfactory number of wickets (that famous "first hour" when the Taunton wicket does unexpected things) and the Wiseacres confined themselves to comments on the play, but when the visiting team had settled down and were playing more defensively and there wasn't so much action, then their conversation turned to other topics. I was delighted to learn that Dora was now out of plaster and responding well to physiotherapy and that North London's daughter in Australia had just had her first child. Then they turned, as they usually do, to what they had seen on television the night before.

"Dreadful thing about that bishop!" MCC said.

"I think I must have missed that," North London replied.

"On the nine o'clock news. A bishop, in the Midlands somewhere, doing something fraudulent with church funds. Couldn't believe my ears! He'd been siphoning off money right, left and center, thousands! He'd been getting away with it for years—well, you wouldn't suspect someone like that, a man of the cloth! Apparently some investments of his own went wrong, a company he'd put a lot of money in went bust or something, and he started to borrow. Well, then, of course, it snowballed from there, downhill all the way. It could never have happened when Fisher was archbishop of Canterbury (wonderful headmaster that man, Nigel was under him at Repton) but now, with all this guitars in churches and bishops called Jim and Dick, what can you expect!"

A small alarm bell at the back of my mind went off and a name suddenly emerged. Crashaw Investments (I'd noticed the name because of the poet)—and I remembered my friend Rosemary's husband Jack saying, about a year ago, how lucky it was that he'd listened to some chap who'd warned him that the company was heading for a crash because they'd *seemed* absolutely rock-solid, but now they were right down the drain. And it was Crashaw Investments (it suddenly came to me) that had featured heavily in the printout of investments on Francis's desk, the printout that Francis hadn't wanted me to see.

Suppose, then, that his financial position had not been as secure as we had been led to believe. I wasn't sure how this affected the problem of his murder, but, taken with the fact that Francis had removed all his affairs (and all the relevant papers) from his solicitor, there was some mystery somewhere. It seemed more imperative than ever that I should talk to Adrian. If anyone knew about Francis's financial affairs he must.

A great burst of applause around the ground, Michael's delighted exclamation "Yes!" and an "Oh, well bowled, sir" from behind recalled me to the present.

"Did you see that yorker!" Michael said. "I think he's broken one of the stumps!"

"Marvelous!" I said.

"He's been very erratic this season," Michael said, "all those no-balls. But it's almost worth it for a ball like that!"

I turned my attention to the game and watched as the bowler, a very tall young man, shirt untucked and flapping, began his run-up, arms held at an odd angle so that he looked like a jet-propelled stick insect. He let fly the ball and the umpire signaled a wide.

After lunch the match slowed down. The spinners came on and the run rate was more static. In one of the longeurs I was idly scanning the crowd near the pavilion when I gave a cry. I handed the binoculars to Michael and said, "Look, just to the right of that steward at the back there, it's Adrian! What's he doing here?"

"I think his firm's one of the sponsors today—yes, come to think of it, I saw their name on the board as we came in. I suppose he had to come—clients to be entertained, corporate hospitality and all that."

"I must go and speak to him," I said, half rising.

Michael grabbed my arm. "Wait till the end of the over, Ma!"

As soon as I could I raced down the steps and around to where I'd seen Adrian. He wasn't there but, by dint of much searching, I spotted him sitting on a bench behind the sight-screen. He looked ill and wretched. I approached cautiously, as if stalking a wild bird, and came up to him suddenly, so that he had no opportunity to see me and make his escape.

"Adrian!" I greeted him. "What a pleasant surprise! No, don't get up," I continued as he made as if to rise and get away. "I'll join you for a moment, if you don't mind. It's nice and cool here out of the sun. Well, I didn't know you were a cricket enthusiast."

He muttered something about being here with the firm.

"Of course. Michael brought me, he's taken a day off because he particularly wanted to see this match ..." I rambled on until his first instinct, for flight, had been overcome by his natural good manners.

"Adrian," I said quietly, "Judy's very worried about you. She's awfully upset that you haven't been in touch."

He turned and gazed at me, panic-stricken. He made as if to say something, but no words came.

"Yes, I've met Judy and I know all about Robert. Adrian," I said earnestly, laying my hand on his arm, "she's deeply fond of you, and very anxious about all this. Look, I'm sure you have your reasons for not seeing her, but do please trust her, give her the chance to understand."

He shook his head. "It's no good," he said. "I can't."

"Adrian, what is it? It can't be as bad as all that!"

The look of desperation in his eyes was frightening. "I can't," he repeated.

"Is there any message I can give her?" I persisted.

"Tell her," he almost whispered, "tell her to forget I ever existed."

He made as if to get up and I said quickly, "Adrian. There is another thing. I don't want to bother you when you're obviously so distressed, but David does need to know how he stands. About the house, I mean. I imagine you're the only person who knows about your father's financial affairs, so if you could just have a word ..."

He stared at me blankly, almost as if he had forgotten who I was. "The house?"

"Yes," I said, "the house on West Hill. I believe David inherits the whole thing now, under the terms of the trust. Who is your solicitor? Who should he get in touch with?"

"In touch with?" he echoed. "I—I'll write to him. I'm sorry, I've got to go now."

He got to his feet and was gone before I could say anything more. I stared after him as he pushed his way through the crowd around the back of the pavilion. Adrian Beaumont was a very disturbed young man and there seemed to be only one reason for his strange behavior.

# 19

So you see," I told David that evening, "I honestly don't know what to say—about who you should get in touch with about the house."

Needless to say we had all discussed ad nauseam Adrian's extraordinary state and had speculated with varying degrees of wildness on Francis's financial position.

"I wonder if he managed to get his hands on Joan's trust fund?" Michael said. "It might just have been possible if he got Adrian to cut a few corners. And that might explain why Adrian's in such a panic now it'll all come out."

"Oh, not that!" I exclaimed. "Joan promised she'd give Mary some of that money to buy her partnership in the stables. If it's all gone ..."

"The trouble is," Michael said, "if Francis didn't appoint another solicitor and if he kept all the paperwork—stuff about investments and so on—in his own hands or did things through Adrian on a sort of ad hoc basis, then, until Adrian applies for probate and chooses to divulge what's been going on, we've no way of knowing *what* the situation is!"

"I'm sure Mary's going to want to know pretty soon about the terms of whatever will he left," I said.

"Yes, well, that's another reason for Adrian to be jumpy," Michael said.

I was still speculating idly on Francis's will and what it might contain at breakfast next day. Michael had gone off early and David and I were sitting over our third cups of coffee, 'slothing around,' as my friend Rosemary calls it. David was listening with half an ear while leafing through the *Daily Telegraph*.

"I suppose we might know more after the funeral," I said. "After all, that is the traditional time to read wills, isn't it?"

"Oh, absolutely ... Good heavens!"

"What is it?"

"Poor old Dickie Davidson's dead. There's an obituary here."

"How sad. I remember how marvelous he was in that Ibsen season, and didn't he do *Heartbreak House* with Marcia Farmer and Julia Grey a couple of years ago? He was a friend of yours, wasn't he?"

"Yes, we were at Nottingham Rep together years ago. It was my first big chance, Constantin in *The Seagull*, and he was playing Trigorin. Constance Whipple was Arkardina and she was the most awful bitch, ego the size of Wembley Stadium. She upstaged me quite *relentlessly* all through rehearsals and I was too green to know how to cope with it. The director didn't dare say a thing because, of course, she was a draw and he didn't dare offend her. But Dickie, who was an even bigger draw in those days, took her to one side and gave her a terrific finger-wagging, after which she was sweetness and light. Bless him! We've always kept in touch. He's been ill off and on for years now and I used to go and see him at Denville Hall. He was quite alone then, his boyfriend, Bobby, died quite young—terribly sad. And then Dickie got this cancer thing and had to go into a hospice. I visited him a couple of times this year, whenever I managed to get up to London."

"Poor thing."

"Yes, it's a merciful release, as they say, because he was in a lot of pain at the end—had to be kept sedated. Oh well, all the old ones are going ..."

"Which reminds me—Francis's funeral. We'll all go, of course, Michael's taking the day off. I imagine Joan will want you to sit with them in the family pew."

It was a very impressive service. Full ecclesiastical honors for the dean in his own cathedral. The bishop spoke well, the choir sang like angels and there was a large and attentive congregation, and yet, as I looked up at the soaring roof, at the vaulting and the gilding, at the banners, moving slightly in the high, thin air, I didn't feel we were mourning a real person. It seemed like a pageant, splendid but formal, and without a heart. Of all the many people in that great building, only one truly grieved for Francis, and that made me very sad.

Because we had to drive David home, Michael and I (reluctantly) went, with a small group of people, back to the deanery after the service and the committal. Joan had arranged for sherry and sandwiches and, as so often happens on these occasions, as the tension lightened, people began to talk more freely and more naturally. There was even the occasional subdued burst of laughter.

I looked around the room for Adrian. He was backed up in a corner by the window with a large, gray-haired man who was talking earnestly to him. Adrian looked ill at ease and seemed to be saying very little in reply. Mary was passing with a plate of sandwiches and I touched her arm.

"Mary, who's that man Adrian's talking to? There, over by the window. I seem to know the face, but I can't put a name to him."

"Oh, that's Donald Gibbons, the cathedral treasurer."

"Oh yes, I thought I knew him. So tell me, how is everything going? About the stables, I mean."

"Well, we can't do much until Adrian sorts out Mother's trust, and she won't let me hurry him over that because he's been so ill." Mary sounded resentful. "Which is all very well, but Fay does need to know how things stand pretty soon."

"Adrian's no better, then?" I asked tentatively.

"Well, he seemed to pull himself together a bit—went back to work and all that. But these last few days he's been worse than ever. In fact, we did wonder if he'd be all right to come to the funeral. Honestly, it doesn't make sense. It isn't as if he'd been fond of Father; he hated him as much as I did! Sorry, that's not the sort of thing I should be saying at a time like this, but it's true and I'd be a hypocrite if I pretended otherwise ..."

She broke off abruptly as Joan came over and joined us. Her black, high-necked dress made her look sallow and old and her eyes were red with recently shed tears. She embraced me warmly.

"Thank you for coming, Sheila, and it was so good of Michael, too."

"It was a beautiful service," I said, "and I thought the bishop spoke splendidly, just the right note. And it was marvelous to see the cathedral so full."

"Yes, people were so kind. Francis would have been very touched. Oh, excuse me, the bishop's leaving, I must just have a word ..."

David came up behind me. "No reading of the will," he said. "Just as we imagined, Joan was rather flustered about that. Actually, darling, now that the bishop's gone I think we might make our getaway ..."

"Hang on a moment, I'd like to have a word with Adrian." I looked round the room, but Adrian had vanished.

"Well, I'm glad there was a good turnout, for Joan's sake," Rosemary said, "and I suppose it was a sort of *occasion*, with the bishop and everything."

"Full ceremonial," I agreed. "Francis would have liked that."

I'd really only gone around to Rosemary's to deliver some jumble, but, as usual, I couldn't resist a cup of coffee and a gossip.

"I mustn't stay long because I haven't been to the shops yet and there's nothing in the house for lunch. Michael won't be in, but David's there, of course, and, although he's the easiest person in the world, it's still one more thing to think about ... Anyway, I can see you're busy." I gestured toward the far end of the sitting room where Delia had set out her dolls in a semicircle and was pouring imaginary tea for them and singing in that high-pitched, otherworldly way that little girls do.

"Oh, Jilly's taking Alex to the clinic and then shopping," Rosemary said, "so I have Delia for the morning. She's very good, really. Except for the nursery rhymes—ever since she started to go to play school she's been singing nonstop."

"And that's bad?"

"It is when you get one of the beastly things on your brain and it won't go away. Last week it was 'The Good Ship Sails on the Ally Ally Oo' and I had it for *days*!"

I laughed. "Oh dear, I wish you hadn't told me—I'm afraid I'm going to have it on my brain now!"

"So, when's David going back to Stratford?" Rosemary asked.

"It's still all up in the air. He can't really leave while the investigation's going on, though I suppose if he *had* to they couldn't stop him. We haven't heard any more from Inspector Hosegood. Has Roger said anything?"

"Well, you know how it is, he doesn't say much, but I gather they've been talking to a lot of people and haven't really got anything concrete."

"Presumably if they had anything they considered hard evidence they'd have hauled David in. Did I tell you that they're considering Nana's death now. They seem to think that might be murder, too."

"Oh, for goodness sake! The poor old soul fell downstairs and I'm not a bit surprised, that house was dark as a tomb, she never put a light on!"

"Exactly. It's perfectly obvious it was an accident, but the inspector had David in and grilled him about going to see her!"

Delia now approached us, one hand extended.

"My dollies has sent you some chocolate cake," she announced.

We both graciously accepted the invisible goodies and she returned to her play, exhorting the dolls to "Row, row, row the boat gently down the stream."

"Talking of accidents," Rosemary said, "I heard from Rosa Harris yesterday—you remember her, that nice American Jack and I met in Venice, terrific traveler."

"Oh yes."

"She was in Egypt with her mother—equally indefatigable although she's well in her eighties—and the mother went down with some sort of acute stomach thing, giardiasis I think it's called, intestinal parasites, really horrible. Fortunately, she had some morphine tablets (you know how some Americans take complete pharmacopoeias with them when they travel!) and she had one tablet and that did the trick. However, the poor old soul is a bit vague, and Rose only just stopped her in time. She'd got the containers mixed up and she was going to put three or four in her coffee—she thought they were sweeteners! Well, they do look very similar. Sheila! Are you all right?"

"No, no," I said, "I'm fine. It's just—I must go now else I'll never get lunch on time."

At the far end of the room Delia was still singing: "Merrily, merrily, merrily, merrily, life is but a dream."

I got into my car and drove down to the seafront. As I sat there, staring at the expanse of unmarked sand, left wet by the retreating tide, I allowed myself to think the unthinkable thoughts that Rosemary's chance remark had prompted. I had a picture of David shaking sweeteners into his coffee. It was all too possible ...

Motive? There was that in abundance. The sale of the house was his last chance to save his own beloved home and to build a new and promising career. Only Francis (and Nana?) stood between him and what he so desperately wanted. Means? He had spoken of visiting his old friend, kept under sedation. There would be medication around ... Opportunity? Well, Francis went out of the room twice while David was there; it would have been easy to put the tablets into the indigestion mixture. The strong peppermint flavor would have disguised any unusual taste. It would have been so easy. The police had suspected him immediately: he was the obvious suspect. It was not inconceivable that the obvious suspect might be the right one.

Far in the distance a man and a woman were walking across the sand, tiny figures, abstract entities, hardly identifiable as human beings. Only as they came nearer was it possible to see them as actual people, to realize that they had feelings and emotions, were capable of thought and action. Delia's song was going echoing in my mind. "Merrily, merrily, merrily, merrily, life is but a dream." But life isn't a dream. Life's not a walking shadow. Life is real, life is earnest, life is an incurable disease ...

The figures on the beach came up the steps and onto the promenade and I recognized them as an elderly couple I knew from the Music Society. They saw me in the car and waved in greeting. Automatically I waved back. David was my dear friend. I had known him all my life. I would trust him with my life. He was the kindest, gentlest, most generous of creatures, incapable of hurting a living soul. There was no way he could commit even a minor crime against another human being. And yet ... If the motive was strong enough, who could be sure that they would not find the temptation too great?

My mind was going around in circles, getting nowhere.

Because I knew I didn't want it to arrive at a conclusion. I started up the car and drove home.

David came into the hall the moment he heard my key in the lock. His face was troubled as he moved toward me and took my hand in his.

"Sheila dear, the most terrible thing has happened. Adrian's tried to kill himself. He's in hospital now—they don't know if they can save him."

# 20

Oh God," I said, "what have I done!"

"Darling, what do you mean? This is nothing to do with you."

"Yes, yes." I broke away from him in agitation. "I confronted Adrian about Judy and the child and I asked him about Francis's finances. Don't you see? He must have known that I'd go on digging, that I'd find out that he killed his father!"

As I spoke, I realized that Adrian's act, terrible as it was and implying a dreadful crime, had released me from my agonizing speculations about David's possible guilt. There could only be one explanation for Adrian's attempted suicide. I tried to pull myself together.

"I'm sorry, David, I was being hysterical. It's just that I'm so afraid I might have pushed him too far."

"You mustn't blame yourself. Look, sit down. Do you want a cup of anything? A drink?"

I shook my head. "Oh, poor Joan! This on top of Francis's death! Did she phone? How did you hear?"

"Mary rang. She was just going back to the hospital, Joan's still there, of course. They found him—well, Joan found him, I'm afraid, this morning. He must have taken the tablets last night."

"Tablets? What tablets?"

"Aspirin, I think, some sort of massive overdose."

"Aspirin?"

"Yes, why?"

"Nothing. Go on."

"Well, they got him to hospital and pumped him out. But they may have been too late, he's still unconscious."

"Oh God," I said wearily, "this is a wretched business."

David leaned forward in his chair. "You think Adrian killed Francis in case he found out about this girl and the baby and made life hell for all of them?"

"Yes, I do. *And* I believe there's something fishy about those shares and all Francis's business dealings, and if there is then Adrian *must* have been involved—Francis would have worked through him, don't you think? And Adrian wouldn't have dared to protest. Now that Francis is dead all that's got to come out, so Adrian's firm is going to find out that he's been doing shady deals for his father. And *that* means he'd lose his job—might even be prosecuted." I sighed. "No wonder that overdose must have seemed the only way out."

"Poor boy," David said gently.

"And no wonder," I continued, "that he told Judy to forget he ever existed. He didn't want her to be dragged into all this. Oh dear, no one else knew of her existence in his life, there was nothing to connect her to him, and then I turned up! It may have been the one thing that pushed him over the edge!"

"No!" David said firmly. "You're not to think like that. If he was going to kill himself he'd have done it anyway, it was nothing to do with you. If he'd killed his father! Well!"

"You may be right, I don't know. It's just that I feel so guilty." I got up from my chair and began to walk about the room. "I wish we knew how Adrian is. I suppose it's no use phoning the hospital?"

"They'll only say he's comfortable or something. Anyway, I expect Mary will ring when there's any news," David said soothingly.

I suddenly thought of something. "I wonder if he left a note?" I asked.

David shook his head. "Mary didn't say, but then she didn't say much at all—just the bare facts."

"I expect she was too upset to go into any details." I stood by the window watching the white clouds drifting slowly across a brilliantly blue sky. "It's a really beautiful day," I said. "That seems to make it worse, somehow."

" 'Fear no more the heat of the sun,' " David quoted softly. He got up and came over to the window and we both stood there in silence for a moment.

"I think I would like a cup of coffee after all," I said. "How about you?"

"Good idea."

Moving about the kitchen making the coffee helped a little and I was grateful too when Foss, coming in through the cat door and bellowing for food, diverted my mind. He jumped up onto the worktop as I was cutting up some cooked chicken, impatiently trying to scoop a piece from under the knife with his paw.

"All right, all right," I said, "I'm being as quick as I can."

Urged on by his strident cries, I put the saucer of food down on the floor and went back into the sitting room with the coffee.

"Here we are then." I handed David his cup and he put it down on a small table while he fished in a pocket for his tube of sweeteners.

"You are being good about those things," I said, thinking how a short time ago they had taken on such a sinister aspect. "Have I weaned you off sugar entirely?"

David shook a couple of small tablets into his cup. "Absolutely," he said smugly. "Even in the face of temptation!"

"Oh?"

"Yes, that day when I had tea with Francis, he put a

couple of lumps of sugar in the cup of tea he poured for me, but even then I didn't succumb!"

"What did you do?"

David looked complacent. "Ah well, Francis had to go out of the room to see someone just after he'd poured the tea—before he'd had time to put sugar in his own cup—so I just changed the cups around and put sweeteners in the one he'd poured for himself and had that."

'You did what!"

David looked at me in surprise. "What's the matter?"

"Don't you realize what you've just said!" I almost shouted.

"What? What do you mean? What's all the excitement about?"

I tried to keep my voice steady. "When Francis came back—he drank the tea? The cup he'd put sugar in?"

"Yes. Yes, he did. Of course he didn't *know* it was that cup—he put another couple of lumps in. It must have been very sweet, even for Francis."

"Of course! That would have hidden any taste! David, why on earth didn't you mention all this before?"

*What* taste? Mention what? Sheila, darling, have you gone completely mad or have I?"

"Think about it," I said. "It wasn't *Francis* who was supposed to die." David looked at me in bewilderment. "Who, then?"

"You, you idiot!"

"But who'd want to ... Oh my God!"

"Exactly."

"You mean, Francis put morphine in my tea to try and kill me?"

"It must have been liquid morphine on those particular lumps of sugar," I said, trying to work it out. "Quite easy to manage, he could have put them to one side before you arrived so that he knew which ones they were. It all falls into place! Naturally, if Francis *had* been the intended victim, then the glass of medicine would have been the obvious place to put the poison, which is why we all focused on that and didn't think of the tea! And, of course, all the tea things had been washed up before anything happened to make people suspicious."

"I wish," David said irritably, "you'd stop theorizing as if this was just an academic exercise! Damn it, I've only just taken in the fact that someone's tried to kill me. Believe me, it's a shaker!"

"Oh, David, I'm sorry. But you do see ... Anyway, if only you'd told us straight away about switching the cups then we'd have known immediately what had happened and you'd have been spared all this police suspicion!"

David shrugged. "I'd completely forgotten it until you went on about the sweeteners. I mean, it was something so trivial, and we all took it for granted that it was Francis who was meant to be killed." He paused and then shook his head in bewilderment. "But why should Francis want to kill me? I mean, we didn't get on, but there are limits!"

"Well, he'd obviously got into really deep water financially, perhaps not just his own money, but cathedral funds as well. I think he needed all the money from the sale of the house, not just his share."

"Good God."

"It was his last resource, you see. He'd used everything else—probably all Joan's money as well. He must have been desperate. Think of it! To have his fraudulent dealings exposed—no longer to be a dean, probably no longer a clergyman either! Francis, who gloried so much in his position, was so scornful of all lesser mortals! And to be spread all over the tabloids, too, like that poor wretched bishop. He couldn't have borne the humiliation."

"But why didn't he just *ask* me?" David said. "I'd have helped somehow."

I smiled pityingly. "Can you imagine Francis admitting—to you of all people—that he'd failed in his financial dealings? The one thing he was supposed to be so brilliant at! And, anyway, Francis didn't understand generosity. It would be quite beyond his comprehension that anyone could be capable of that sort of unselfishness."

"But murder! It's unbelievable!"

"You were right," I said, "when you said it was like a Jacobean tragedy. Fratricide is particularly Websterian, and by poison too!"

"But then," David said, "what about Adrian? Why the overdose?"

"I don't know, but I'm pretty sure he knew about the money, so perhaps he suspected about the murder too."

"Oh God."

"So that when Francis died, he knew his suspicions had been right but that something had gone terribly wrong. No wonder he broke down like that."

"But look," David said, "if Francis was going to poison me that teatime, surely he'd have been the main suspect?"

"Not really. I think he must have got the dose of morphine wrong. I imagine the idea was that you'd come back here and die quietly in your sleep. Death from natural causes. Besides, what possible motive could the dean of Culminster have for killing his brother?"

David sighed. "I'm sure you're right, but I still can't take it in."

"Come to think of it, if Francis had judged the amount of morphine correctly then *he* would have died in his sleep instead of being discovered in a coma and rushed to hospital, and it's just possible that no one would have thought of murder.

David sat back in his chair. "So what are we going to do? Tell the police?"

"I think we must, don't you?"

"I don't like the idea of being the one to, well, bring disgrace on Francis ..."

"David! This is no time to be quixotic! He tried to kill you, for God's sake! Anyway, I have a feeling that other people in the cathedral are beginning to get suspicious about the money. I'm afraid there's no way of saving his good name now—even to spare Joan and Mary."

"I know what you mean, darling," David said reluctantly, "it's just that I wish I didn't have to be the one to do it."

I got up to clear away the coffee cups and as I was taking them out to the kitchen the phone rang. It was Mary.

"Just to let you know that Adrian's all right and they're letting us take him home."

"Thank God! Oh Mary, I'm so glad!" I paused. "Do you know," I asked tentatively, "what happened?"

"Why he did it, you mean? No, not really. He didn't leave any sort of note and he's still very weak, so we can't talk to him about it yet."

"No, of course. Give my love to your mother. How is she?"

"Still very shaken, but very relieved—you can imagine."

"Yes, well, if there's anything we can do ..."

"Well, actually there is. I don't know why, but Adrian's insisting on seeing you and David right away. We tried to make him wait until he's stronger but he got so agitated ... He said it was a matter of life and death. Does any of it make sense to you?"

"Yes," I said. "I think it does. Look, I've just got a phone call to make and then we'll be over right away."

Adrian was sitting up in bed looking pale and drawn, which was not surprising, but also quite calm, which was. David and I sat down on the chairs that Mary had put on either side of the bed. David looked at me inquiringly and I began.

"We're so glad you're all right, Adrian. I'd never have forgiven myself if anything had happened." He made a movement to speak and I continued quickly. "We know about your father. We know about his financial difficulties. We know that he tried to kill David. It isn't a secret you have to keep any longer."

Adrian gave a great shuddering sob and buried his face in his hands.

"It's all right, Adrian," I said gently. "It's all over."

He looked up imploringly at David. "I didn't *know* he was going to kill you—it was, well, just some of the things he said, about settling things and the situation changing, that made me wonder. Part of me couldn't believe that he'd do such a thing, but part of me ... Oh God, I *should* have said something! You could have died. But I was so afraid of him! When he died I couldn't think what had happened, how it had happened, I was so *relieved*, but so guilty at feeling relieved. You can't imagine! I was free of him at last, but with this terrible secret. How can you ever forgive me?"

David laid his hand on Adrian's. "It's all right. I understand," he said.

Adrian went on, the words tumbling out now as if he couldn't tell the whole story fast enough. "It wasn't only that. I've let them down, too, Mother and Mary. The money's gone. Father made me break Mother's trust so that he could get at the money—now that's all gone, too. And that's not the worst! There's money from the cathedral funds—I don't know how much, I never knew what he was doing there—there'll be the most terrible scandal!"

"Yes, we guessed that," I said. "That was why he needed all the money from the house sale, wasn't it? That's why he needed to kill David?"

"That wasn't the only reason," Adrian said. He paused and then brought out the words painfully. "He'd signed the contract to sell to this developer—he forged your signature, Uncle David."

"But"—David looked bewildered—"he told me that the time wasn't right to sell."

"That was to keep you away from the whole business until he ..."

"Until he could get rid of me?"

"Yes. I suppose that was when I realized what he meant to do."

"That was the step too far," I said. "There was no going back after that."

"I didn't feel I could bear to live with myself," Adrian said, his voice hoarse with exhaustion and emotion. "There seemed to be no way out. And then there was Judy and Robbie—I couldn't bear Judy to know what I'd done. I wanted to give them a clean break so that they could get on with their lives without my awful ... without what I'd done overshadowing them."

"It was very wrong of you to try and take your own life," I said. "Judy is strong, she has the right to know and to make her own decision."

"But I must tell the police," Adrian said vehemently, "and the cathedral authorities—the treasurer is suspicious, I think. I may be prosecuted. I can't ask her to forgive all this."

The door opened and Mary put her head around.

"The visitor you told me about, Sheila, has arrived. Shall I show her in?"

I nodded and looked at David and we both got up and went toward the door as Judy came in. She went over to the bed, looked down at Adrian and said, "You really are a complete bloody fool!" Then she put her arms around him and laid her cheek against his hair, stroking it as he cried as if his heart would break.

# 21

So it doesn't look as if Adrian is going to be prosecuted," I said. "The police can't really *prove* that he knew what his father intended to do, and presumably you wouldn't bring charges against him?"

"Good God, no!" David exclaimed.

"I gather from Roger that Inspector Hosegood is a bit miffed about the whole thing—I can see that it's not a very satisfactory solution from the police point of view. Adrian's lost his job, of course, but Judy's going to teach him how to be a computer programmer. He's moved in with her now and Joan's going to live with Evelyn Burgess. Do you know, Francis must have stolen some of poor old Canon Burgess's morphine when he went to visit him on his deathbed, isn't that unspeakable! And, of course, Evelyn is so vague she thought that the district nurse had taken the remainder away and didn't realize."

David and I were back in Stratford, sitting in the Pizza Hut chatting over a late lunch. I had originally expressed surprise at David's choice of venue, but he said that he'd got into the habit of lunching there with his lodgers. "Such a good place to bring the young, darling," he said, indicating a notice that said, "All the pizza and salad you can eat for £4.99."

"I'm going to give Joan the money for Francis's share of the house," he said.

"Oh, David, that's incredibly generous of you!"

"Well, the cathedral people have been very good. Obviously *they* don't want a scandal any more than we do, so the treasurer chap said that if the money was paid back—in view of what's happened—they'd quietly forget the whole thing. So the Beaumont name won't be dishonored! And there should be a bit left over for Mary's stable thing."

"You're too good to be true!" I smiled at him affectionately.

"We-ell. I've got enough from my share of the house for what I need—and I must say, Francis did a really good deal, he got a fantastic price—and, now that splendid Beth Cameron has confirmed my appointment as head of the study center, I shall have everything in the world that I want!"

"Not many people can say that."

"The only thing that worries me," David said, "is poor old Nana. Do you think Francis really did push her downstairs?" This remark, uttered in David's resonant actor's voice, caused a woman with two small children at the next table to turn and eye us apprehensively.

I shrugged my shoulders. "We shall never know now. Adrian obviously had no sort of suspicion that her death wasn't an accident, so Francis couldn't have said anything to him about it. I think, on balance, that it was. After all, she was pretty tottery and those stairs were always badly lit, so try not to brood about it."

"Actually, I'm going to be so busy soon that I won't have time to brood about anything. Now then, when's this chap Mike arriving?"

I was in Stratford because one of my American friends was visiting and wanted me to show him around. "He's coming on the twelve-thirty London train tomorrow."

"I suppose," David said resignedly, "you'll want to take him to Wilmcote to share in your lovefest with those terrible birds?"

I thought of the hawks, handsome, ruthless, single-minded in pursuit of their prey, and I thought of Francis. I shivered. "I don't know," I said, "there may not be time."

"Oh well," David replied, "there's always masses to show him in the town, goodness knows!"

He gestured to a plaque on the wall informing the curious that this fine Tudor house, one of the oldest in Stratford (now alas, inside at least, in the red and chrome uniform of the pizza chain) had been restored by the writer Marie Corelli.

"You do know," he said, "that she had a gondola with a gondolier, specially imported from Italy, to row her up and down the Avon."

"How lovely."

"Actually, I know a man who nearly bought it. He went to a country house sale at Shottery, just after the war, and there it was."

"But he didn't buy it?"

"He was very tempted, but, as he said, he'd nowhere to put it, so it would have just sat in the garden and quietly rotted away. The way things do, you know."

"Yes," I said. "I know."

David moved an olive stone around the rim of his plate with the tip of his knife.

"Sheila," he said, not looking up, "there's something I must tell you."

"What is it?" I asked, slightly bewildered by his sudden change of mood.

"It's just that—oh God, this is so *difficult*!" He looked up at last and said, "When I went to see Nana that time—you know—she was already dead."

"What!"

"I found her there in the hall. She'd obviously fallen down the stairs. She was quite dead."

"And you left her there?"

"Oh God, I know—it sounds so awful—but I panicked. I

knew how suspicious it would look—I simply lost my head and got out as fast as I could."

"But how did you get in, if she was ..."

"I rang the bell and there was no answer so I went around to the side door and that was open so I just walked in. I called out but of course there was no reply, so I went into the hall and there she was."

He buried his face in his hands. "The times I've seen her since then, lying there ..."

"But how could you? She might have lain there for days!"

"I know, I know! But once I'd done it, then it seemed impossible to tell anyone. I was so ashamed! I tried to rationalize it—there was a bottle of milk by the side door, I told myself the milkman would see it the next day and investigate—actually, that's what did happen, Francis told me. I felt a bit better after that."

"Oh, David."

"And then, all that business with Francis and the police and everything. You do see, don't you?"

I nodded.

"I'm afraid I'm not a very strong person. Francis had all the decisiveness in our family. I know it was a feeble thing to do—a rotten thing to do—but, well ..."

He looked at me appealingly. Dear David. Perhaps I would never feel quite the same about him again, but all those years of friendship and fondness bound us with strong ties. And I did understand.

"Of course I see," I said. "I'd probably have done exactly the same thing myself."

David gave me a wry, lopsided smile, his Inspector Ivor smile.

"Perhaps," he said, "perhaps."

**Mrs. Malory Mysteries**

**Published by Coffeetown Press**

*Gone Away*, or *Mrs. Malory Investigates* (1989)

*The Cruellest Month* (1991)

*The Shortest Journey*, or
*Mrs. Malory's Shortest Journey* (1992)

*Mrs. Malory and the Festival Murder*, or
*Uncertain Death* (1993)

*Murder on Campus*, or *Detective in Residence* (1994)

*Superfluous Death*, or *Mrs. Malory Wonders Why* (1995)

*Death of a Dean* (1996)

**Other Mysteries by Hazel Holt**

**Published by Coffeetown Press**

*My Dear Charlotte* (2010)

**Hazel Holt** was born in Birmingham, England, where she attended King Edward VI High School for Girls. She studied at Newnham College, Cambridge, and went on to work at the International African Institute in London, where she became acquainted with the novelist Barbara Pym, whose biography she later wrote. She also finished one of Pym's novels after Pym died. Holt has also recently published *My Dear Charlotte*, a story that uses the actual language of Jane Austen's letters to her sister Cassandra to construct a Regency murder mystery. Holt wrote her first novel in her sixties, and is a leading crime novelist. She is best known for her Mrs. Malory series. Her son is novelist Tom Holt.

CPSIA information can be obtained at www.ICGtesting.com
Printed in the USA
LVOW10s2348100713

342359LV00001B/24/P